Praise for *Eastern Standard Tribe*

"Cory Doctorow is just far enough ahead of the game to give you the authentic chill of the future. . . . Funny as hell and sharp as steel."
—Warren Ellis, author of *Transmetropolitan*

"Immediately accessible . . . Doctorow maintains an unrelenting pace; many readers will find themselves finishing the novel, as I did, in a single sitting."
—*Toronto Star*

"At its heart, *Tribe* is a witty, sometimes acerbic poke in the eye at modern culture. Everything comes under Doctorow's microscope, and he manages to be both up-to-date and off-the-cuff in the best possible way."
—*Locus*

"As in *Down and Out,* Doctorow shows here that he's got the modern world, in all its Googled, Friendstered, and PDA-d glory, completely sussed."
—*Kirkus Reviews*

"John W. Campbell Award winner Doctorow lives up to the promise of his first novel. . . . This short novel's occasionally bitter, sometimes hilarious, and always wackily appealing protagonist consistently skewers those evils of modern culture he holds most pernicious."
—*Publishers Weekly*

"Cory Doctorow knocks me out. In a good way."
—Pat Cadigan, author of *Synners*

cory doctorow: **eastern standard tribe**

A Tom Doherty Associates Book
TOR® New York

EASTERN STANDARD TRIBE

Edited by Patrick Nielsen Hayden

Book design by Michael Collica

A Tor Book
Published by Tom Doherty Associates, LLC
175 Fifth Avenue
New York, NY 10010

www.tor.com

Tor® is a registered trademark of Tom Doherty Associates, LLC.

Library of Congress Cataloging-in-Publication Data

Doctorow, Cory.
    Eastern standard tribe / Cory Doctorow.
        p. cm.
    "A Tom Doherty Associates book."
    ISBN 0-765-31045-7
    EAN 978-0765-31045-3
    1. Time—Systems and standards—Fiction. 2. Business consultants—Fiction. 3. Americans—Europe—Fiction. 4. Secret societies—Fiction. 5. Sleep-wake cycle—Fiction. 6. Conspiracies—Fiction. 7. Young men—Fiction. 8. Europe—Fiction. I. Title.

PS3604.O27E23 2004
813'.6—dc22   2003057055

First Hardcover Edition: March 2004
First Trade Paperback Edition: April 2005

Printed in the United States of America

0 9 8 7 6 5 4 3 2 1

For my parents

For my family

For everyone who helped me up and for everyone I let down. You know who you are. Sincerest thanks and most heartfelt apologies.

eastern standard tribe

I once had a Tai Chi instructor who explained the difference between Chinese and Western medicine thus: "Western medicine is based on corpses, things that you discover by cutting up dead bodies and pulling them apart. Chinese medicine is based on living flesh, things observed from vital, moving humans."

The explanation, like all good propaganda, is stirring and stilted, and not particularly accurate, and gummy as the hook from a top-40 song, sticky in your mind in the sleep-deprived noontime when the world takes on a hallucinatory hyperreal clarity. Like now as I sit here in my underwear on the roof of a sanatorium in the backwoods off Route 128, far enough from the perpetual construction of Boston that it's merely a cloud of dust like a herd of distant buffalo charging the plains. Like now as I sit here with a pencil up my nose, thinking about homebrew lobotomies and wouldn't it be nice if I gave myself one.

Deep breath.

The difference between Chinese medicine and Western medicine is the dissection versus the observation of the thing in motion. The difference between reading a story and studying a story is the difference between living the story and killing the story and looking at its guts.

School! We sat in English class and we dissected the stories that I'd escaped into, laid open their abdomens and tagged their organs, covered their genitals with polite, sterile drapes, recorded dutiful notes en masse that told us what the story was about, but never what the story *was*. Stories are propaganda, virii that slide past your critical immune system and insert themselves directly into your emotions. Kill them and cut them open and they're as naked as a nightclub in daylight.

The theme. The first step in dissecting a story is euthanizing it: "What is the theme of this story?"

Let me kill my story before I start it, so that I can dissect it and understand it. The theme of this story is: "Would you rather be smart or happy?"

This is a work of propaganda. It's a story about choosing smarts over happiness. Except if I give the pencil a push: then it's a story about choosing happiness over smarts. It's a morality play, and the first character is about to take the stage. He's a foil for the theme, so he's drawn in simple lines. Here he is:

Art Berry was born to argue.

There are born assassins. Bred to kill, raised on cunning and speed, they are the stuff of legend, remorseless and unstoppable. There are born ballerinas, confectionery girls whose parents subject them to rigors every bit as intense as the tripwire and poison on which the assassins are reared. There are children born to practice medicine or law; children born to serve their nations and die heroically in the noble tradition of their forebears; children born to tread the boards or shred the turf or leave smoking rubber on the racetrack.

Art's earliest memory: a dream. He is stuck in the waiting room of one of the innumerable doctors who attended him in his infancy. He is perhaps three, and his attention span is already as robust as it will ever be, and in his dream—which is fast becoming a nightmare—he is bored silly.

The only adornment in the waiting room is an empty cylinder that once held toy blocks. Its label colorfully illustrates the blocks, which look like they'd be a hell of a lot of fun, if someone hadn't lost them all.

Near the cylinder is a trio of older children, infinitely

fascinating. They confer briefly, then do *something* to the cylinder, and it unravels, extruding into the third dimension, turning into a stack of blocks.

Aha! thinks Art, on waking. This is another piece of the secret knowledge that older people possess, the strange magic that is used to operate cars and elevators and shoelaces.

Art waits patiently over the next year for a grown-up to show him how the blocks-from-pictures trick works, but none ever does. Many other mysteries are revealed, each one more disappointingly mundane than the last: even flying a plane seemed easy enough when the nice stew let him ride up in the cockpit for a while en route to New York—Art's awe at the complexity of adult knowledge fell away. By the age of five, he was stuck in a sort of perpetual terrible twos, fearlessly shouting "no" at the world's every rule, arguing the morals and reason behind them until the frustrated adults whom he was picking on gave up and swatted him or told him that that was just how it was.

In the Easter of his sixth year, an itchy-suited and hard-shoed visit to church with his Gran turned into a raging holy war that had the parishioners and the clergy arguing with him in teams and relays.

It started innocently enough: "Why does God care if we take off our hats, Gran?" But the nosy ladies in the nearby pews couldn't bear to simply listen in, and the argument spread like ripples on a pond, out as far as the pulpit, where the priest decided to squash the whole line of inquiry with some half-remembered philosophical word games from Descartes in which the objective truth of reality is used to prove the beneficence of God and vice versa, and culminates with "I think therefore I am." Father Ferlenghetti even managed to work it into the thread of the sermon, but before he could go on, Art's shrill little voice answered from within the congregation.

Amazingly, the six-year-old had managed to assimilate all of Descartes's fairly tricksy riddles in as long as it took to describe them, and then went on to use those same arguments to prove the necessary cruelty of God, followed by the necessary nonexistence of the Supreme Being, and Gran tried to take him home then, but the priest—who'd watched Jesuits play intellectual table tennis and recognized a natural when he saw one—called him to the pulpit, whence Art took on the entire congregation, singly and in bunches, as they assailed his reasoning and he built it back up, laying rhetorical traps that they blundered into with all the cunning of a cabbage. Father Ferlenghetti laughed and clarified the points when they were stuttered out by some marble-mouthed rhetorical amateur from the audience, then sat back and marveled as Art did his thing. Not much was getting done vis-à-vis sermonizing, and there was still the Communion to be administered, but God knew it had been a long time since the congregation was engaged so thoroughly with coming to grips with God and what their faith meant.

Afterwards, when Art was returned to his scandalized, thin-lipped Gran, Father Ferlenghetti made a point of warmly embracing her and telling her that Art was welcome at his pulpit any time, and suggested a future in the seminary. Gran was amazed, and blushed under her Sunday powder, and the clawed hand on his shoulder became a caress.

>>>>>>>>>>>3

The theme of this story is choosing smarts over happiness, or maybe happiness over smarts. Art's a good guy. He's smart as hell. That's his schtick. If he were a cartoon character, he'd be the pain-in-the-ass poindexter who is all the time dispelling the mysteries that fascinate his buddies. It's not easy being Art's friend.

Which is, of course, how Art ("not his real name") ended up sitting forty-five stories over the woodsy Massachusetts countryside, hot August wind ruffling his hair and blowing up the legs of his boxers, pencil in his nose, euthanizing his story preparatory to dissecting it. In order to preserve the narrative integrity, Art ("not his real name") may take some liberties with the truth. This is autobiographical fiction, after all, not an autobiography.

Call me Art ("not my real name"). I am an agent-provocateur in the Eastern Standard Tribe, though

I've spent most of my life in GMT-8 and at various latitudes of Zulu, which means that my poor pineal gland has all but forgotten how to do its job without that I drown it in melatonin precursors and treat it to multi-hour nine-kilolumen sessions in the glare of my travel lantern.

The tribes are taking over the world. You can track our progress by the rise of minor traffic accidents. The sleep-deprived are terrible, terrible drivers. Daylight savings time is a widowmaker: stay off the roads on Leap Forward day!

Here is the second character in the morality play. She's the love interest. Was. We broke up, just before I got sent to the sanatorium. Our circadians weren't compatible.

>>>>>>>>>>>**4**

April 3, 2022 was the day that Art nearly killed the first and only woman he ever really loved. It was her fault.

Art's car was running low on lard after a week in the Benelux countries, where the residents were all high-net-worth cholesterol-conscious codgers who guarded their arteries from the depredations of the frytrap as jealously as they squirreled their money away from the taxman. He was, therefore, thrilled and delighted to be back on British soil, Greenwich+0, where grease ran like water and his runabout could be kept easily and cheaply fuelled and the vodka could run down his gullet instead of into his tank.

He was in the Kensington High Street on a sleepy Sunday morning, BST0300h—2100h back in EST—and the GPS was showing insufficient data-points to even gauge traffic between his geoloc and the Camden High where he kept his rooms. When the GPS can't find enough peers on the relay network to color its maps with traffic data, you know you've hit a sweet spot in the city's uber-circadian, a moment of grace where the roads are very nearly exclusively yours.

So he whistled a jaunty tune and swilled his coffium, a fad that had just made it to the UK, thanks to the loosening of rules governing the disposal of heavy water in the EU. The java just wouldn't cool off, remaining hot enough to guarantee optimal caffeine osmosis right down to the last drop.

If he was jittery, it was no more so than was customary for ESTalists at GMT+0, and he was driving safely and with due caution. If the woman had looked out before stepping off the kerb and into the anemically thin road, if she hadn't been wearing stylish black in the pitchy dark of the curve before the Royal Garden Hotel, if she hadn't stepped *right in front of his runabout*, he would have merely swerved and sworn and given her a bit of a fright.

But she didn't, she was, she did, and he kicked the brake as hard as he could, twisted the wheel likewise, and still clipped her hipside and sent her ass-over-teakettle before the runabout did its own barrel roll, making three complete revolutions across the Kensington High before lodging in the Royal Garden Hotel's shrubs. Art was covered in scorching, molten coffium, screaming and clawing at his eyes, upside down, when the porters from the Royal Garden opened his runabout's upside-down door, undid his safety harness and pulled him out from behind the rapidly flacciding airbag. They plunged his face into the ornamental birdbath, which had a skin of ice that shattered on his nose and jangled against his jawbone as the icy water cooled the coffium and stopped the terrible, terrible burning.

He ended up on his knees, sputtering and blowing and shivering, and cleared his eyes in time to see the woman he'd hit being carried out of the middle of the road on a human travois made of the porters' linked arms of red wool and gold brocade.

"Assholes!" she was hollering. "I could have a goddamn spinal injury! You're not supposed to move me!"

"Look, miss," one porter said, a young chap with the kind of fantastic dentition that only an insecure teabag would ever pay for, teeth so white and flawless they strobed in the sodium streetlamps. "Look. We can leave you in the middle of the road, right, and not move you, like we're supposed to. But if we do that, chances are you're going to get run over before the paramedics get here, and then you certainly *will* have a spinal injury, and a crushed skull besides, like as not. Do you follow me?"

"You!" she said, pointing a long and accusing finger at Art. "You! Don't you watch where you're going, you fool! You could have killed me!"

Art shook water off his face and blew a mist from his dripping moustache. "Sorry," he said, weakly. She had an American accent, Californian maybe, a litigious stridency that tightened his sphincter like an alum enema and miraculously flensed him of the impulse to argue.

"Sorry?" she said, as the porters lowered her gently to the narrow strip of turf beside the sidewalk. "Sorry? Jesus, is that the best you can do?"

"Well you *did* step out in front of my car," he said, trying to marshal some spine.

She attempted to sit up, then slumped back down, wincing. "You were going too fast!"

"I don't think so," he said. "I'm pretty sure I was doing forty-five—that's five clicks under the limit. Of course, the GPS will tell for sure."

At the mention of empirical evidence, she seemed to lose interest in being angry. "Give me a phone, will you?"

Mortals may be promiscuous with their handsets, but for a tribalist, one's relationship with one's comm is deeply personal. Art would have sooner shared his underwear. But he *had* hit her with his car. Reluctantly, Art passed her his comm.

The woman stabbed at the handset with the fingers of her left hand, squinting at it in the dim light. Eventually, she clamped it to her head. "Johnny? It's Linda. Yes, I'm still in London. How's tricks out there? Good, good to hear. How's Marybeth? Oh, that's too bad. Want to hear how I am?" She grinned devilishly. "I just got hit by a car. No, just now. Five minutes ago. Of course I'm hurt! I think he broke my hip—maybe my spine, too. Yes, I can wiggle my toes. Maybe he shattered a disc and it's sawing through the cord right now. Concussion? Oh, almost certainly. Pain and suffering, loss of enjoyment of life, missed wages . . ." She looked up at Art. "You're insured, right?"

Art nodded, miserably, fishing for an argument that would not come.

"Half a mil, easy. Easy! Get the papers going, will you? I'll call you when the ambulance gets here. Bye. Love you too. Bye. Bye. Bye, Johnny. I got to go. Bye!" She made a kissy noise and tossed the comm back at Art. He snatched it out of the air in a panic, closed its cover reverentially and slipped it back in his jacket pocket.

"C'mere," she said, crooking a finger. He knelt beside her.

"I'm Linda," she said, shaking his hand, then pulling it to her chest.

"Art," Art said.

"Art. Here's the deal, Art. It's no one's fault, OK? It

was dark, you were driving under the limit, I was proceeding with due caution. Just one of those things. But *you* did hit *me*. Your insurer's gonna have to pay out—rehab, pain and suffering, you get it. That's going to be serious kwan. I'll go splits with you, you play along."

Art looked puzzled.

"Art. Art. Art. Art, here's the thing. Maybe you were distracted. Lost. Not looking. Not saying you were, but maybe. Maybe you were, and if you were, my lawyer's going to get that out of you, he's going to nail you, and I'll get a big, fat check. On the other hand, you could just, you know, cop to it. Play along. You make this easy, we'll make this easy. Split it down the middle, once my lawyer gets his piece. Sure, your premiums'll go up, but there'll be enough to cover both of us. Couldn't you use some ready cash? Lots of zeroes. Couple hundred grand, maybe more. I'm being nice here—I could keep it all for me."

"I don't think—"

"Sure you don't. You're an honest man. I understand, Art. Art. Art, I understand. But what has your insurer done for you, lately? My uncle Ed, he got caught in a threshing machine, paid his premiums every week for forty years, what did he get? Nothing. Insurance companies. They're the great satan. No one likes an insurance company. Come on, Art. Art. You don't have to say anything now, but think about it, OK, Art?"

She released his hand, and he stood. The porter

with the teeth flashed them at him. "Mad," he said, "just mad. Watch yourself, mate. Get your solicitor on the line, I were you."

He stepped back as far as the narrow sidewalk would allow and fired up his comm and tunneled to a pseudonymous relay, bouncing the call off a dozen mixmasters. He was, after all, in deep cover as a GMTalist, and it wouldn't do to have his enciphered packets' destination in the clear—a little traffic analysis and his cover'd be blown. He velcroed the keyboard to his thigh and started chording.

Trepan: Any UK solicitors on the channel?

Gink-Go: Lawyers. Heh. Kill 'em all. Specially eurofag fixers.

Junta: Hey, I resemble that remark

Trepan: Junta, you're a UK lawyer?

Gink-Go: Use autocounsel, dude. L{ialawye}rs suck. Channel #autocounsel. Chatterbot with all major legal systems on the backend.

Trepan: Whatever. I need a human lawyer.

Trepan: Junta, you there?

Gink-Go: Off raping humanity.

Gink-Go: Fuck lawyers.

Trepan: /shitlist Gink-Go

##Gink-Go added to Trepan's shitlist. Use '/unshit Gink-Go' to see messages again

Gink-Go: <shitlisted>

Gink-Go: <shitlisted>

Gink-Go: <shitlisted>

Gink-Go: <shitlisted>

##Gink-Go added to Junta's shitlist. Use '/unshit Gink-Go'
    to see messages again

##Gink-Go added to Thomas-hawk's shitlist. Use '/unshit
    Gink-Go' to see messages again

##Gink-Go added to opencolon's shitlist. Use '/unshit
    Gink-Go' to see messages again

##Gink-Go added to jackyardbackoff's shitlist. Use '/unshit
    Gink-Go' to see messages again

##Gink-Go added to freddy-kugel's shitlist. Use '/unshit
    Gink-Go' to see messages again

opencolon: Trolls suck. Gink-Go away.

Gink-Go: <shitlisted>

Gink-Go: <shitlisted>

Gink-Go: <shitlisted>

##Gink-Go has left channel #EST.chatter

Junta: You were saying?

##Junta (private) (file transfer)

##Received credential from Junta. Verifying. Credential
    identified: ''Solicitor, registered with the Law Soci-
    ety to practice in England and Wales, also registered
    in Australia.''

Trepan: /private Junta I just hit a woman while driving
    the Kensington High Street. Her fault. She's hurt.
    Wants me to admit culpability in exchange for half
    the insurance. Advice?

##Junta (private): I beg your pardon?

Trepan: /private Junta She's crazy. She just got off the
    phone with some kinda lawyer in the States. Says she

can get $5*10^5$ at least, and will split with me if I
don't dispute.

##Junta (private): Bloody Americans. No offense. What kind
of instrumentation recorded it?

Trepan: /private Junta My GPS. Maybe some secams. Eyewit-
nesses, maybe.

##Junta (private): And you'll say what, exactly? That you
were distracted? Fiddling with something?

Trepan: /private Junta I guess.

##Junta (private): You're looking at three points off your
licence. Statutory increase in premiums totalling EU
$2*10^5$ over five years. How's your record?

##Transferring credential "Driving record" to Junta.
Receipt confirmed.

##Junta (private): Hmmm.

##Junta (private): Nothing outrageous. _Were_ you dis-
tracted?

Trepan: /private Junta I guess. Maybe.

##Junta (private): You guess. Well, who would know better
than you, right? My fee's 10 percent. Stop guessing.
You _were_ distracted. Overtired. It's late. Regret-
table. Sincerely sorry. Have her solicitor contact me
directly. I'll meet you here at 1000h BST/0500h EDT
and go over it with you, yes? Agreeable?

Trepan: /private Junta Agreed. Thanks.

##Junta (private) (file transfer)

##Received smartcontract from Junta. Verifying. Smartcon-
tract "Representation agreement" verified.

Trepan: /join #autocounsel

counselbot: Welcome, Trepan! How can I help you?

##Transferring smartcontract ''Representation agreement'' to counselbot. Receipt confirmed.

Trepan: /private counselbot What is the legal standing of this contract?

##counselbot (private): Smartcontract ''Representation agreement'' is an ISO standard representation agreement between a client and a solicitor for purposes of litigation in the UK.

##autocounsel (private) (file transfer)

##Received ''representation agreement faq uk 2.3.2 2JAN22'' from autocounsel.

Trepan: /join #EST.chatter

Trepan: /private Junta It's a deal

##Transferring key-signed smartcontract ''Representation agreement'' to Junta. Receipt confirmed.

Trepan: /quit Gotta go, thanks!

##Trepan has left channel #EST.chatter ''Gotta go, thanks!''

>>>>>>>>>>>5

Once the messy business of negotiating EU healthcare for foreign nationals had been sorted out with the EMTs and the Casualty Intake triage, once they'd both been digested and shat out by a dozen diagnostic devices, from X-rays to MRIs, once the harried house officers had impersonally prodded them and presented them both with hardcopy FAQs for their various injuries (second-degree burns, mild shock for Art; pelvic dislocation, minor kidney bruising, broken femur, whiplash, concussion and mandible trauma for Linda), they found themselves in adjacent beds in the recovery room, which bustled as though it, too, were working on GMT-5, busy as a 9PM restaurant on a Saturday night.

Art had an IV taped to the inside of his left arm, dripping saline and tranqs, making him logy and challenging his circadians. Still, he was the more mobile of the two, as Linda was swaddled in smartcasts that both immobilized her and massaged her, all the while osmosing transdermal anti-inflammatories and painkillers. He tottered the two steps to the chair at her bedside and shook her hand again.

"Don't take this the wrong way, but you look like hell," he said.

She smiled. Her jaw made an audible pop. "Get a picture, will you? It'll be good in court."

He chuckled.

"No, seriously. Get a picture."

So he took out his comm and snapped a couple pix, including one with nightvision filters on to compensate for the dimmed recovery room lighting. "You're a cool customer, you know that?" he said as he tucked his camera away.

"Not so cool. This is all a coping strategy. I'm pretty shook up, you want to know the truth. I could have died."

"What were you doing on the street at three AM anyway?"

"I was upset, so I took a walk, thought I'd get something to eat or a beer or something."

"You haven't been here long, huh?"

She laughed, and it turned into a groan. "What the hell is wrong with the English, anyway? The sun sets and the city rolls up its streets. It's not like they've got this great tradition of staying home and surfing cable or anything."

"They're all snug in their beds, farting away their lentil roasts."

"That's it! You can't get a steak here to save your life. Mad cows, all of 'em. If I see one more gray soy sausage, I'm going to kill the waitress and eat *her*."

"You just need to get hooked up," he said. "Once we're out of here, I'll take you out for a genuine blood pudding, roast beef and oily chips. I know a place."

"I'm drooling. Can I borrow your phone again? Uh, I think you're going to have to dial for me."

"That's OK. Give me the number."

She did, and he cradled his comm to her head. He was close enough to her that he could hear the tinny, distinctive ringing of a namerican circuit at the other end. He heard her shallow breathing, heard her jaw creak. He smelled her shampoo, a free-polymer new-car smell, smelled a hint of her sweat. A cord stood out on her neck, merging in an elegant vee with her collarbone, an arrow pointing at the swell of her breast under her paper gown.

"Toby, it's Linda."

A munchkin voice chittered down the line.

"Shut up, OK. Shut up. Shut. I'm in the hospital."
More chipmunk. "Got hit by a car. I'll be OK. No.
Shut up. I'll be fine. I'll send you the FAQs. I just
wanted to say . . ." She heaved a sigh, closed her eyes.
"You know what I wanted to say. Sorry, all right?
Sorry it came to this. You'll be OK. I'll be OK. I just
didn't want to leave you hanging." She sounded
groggy, but there was a sob there, too. "I can't talk
long. I'm on a shitload of dope. Yes, it's good dope. I'll
call you later. I don't know when I'm coming back,
but we'll sort it out there, all right? OK. Shut up. OK.
You too."

She looked up at Art. "My boyfriend. Ex-boyfriend.
Not sure who's leaving whom at this point. Thanks."
She closed her eyes. Her eyelids were mauve, a trac-
ery of pink veins. She snored softly.

Art set an alarm that would wake him up in time to
meet his lawyer, folded up his comm and crawled
back into bed. His circadians swelled and crashed
against the sides of his skull, and before he knew it,
he was out.

Hospitals operate around the clock, but they still have their own circadians. The noontime staff were still overworked and harried but chipper and efficient, too, without the raccoon-eyed jitters of the night before. Art and Linda were efficiently fed, watered and evacuated, then left to their own devices, blinking in the weak English sunlight that streamed through the windows.

"The lawyers've worked it out, I think," Art said.

"Good. Good news." She was dopamine-heavy, her words lizard-slow. Art figured her temper was drugged senseless, and it gave him the courage to ask her the question that'd been on his mind since they'd met.

"Can I ask you something? It may be offensive."

"G'head. I may be offended."

"Do you do . . . this . . . a lot? I mean, the insurance thing?"

She snorted, then moaned. "It's the Los Angeles Lottery, dude. I haven't done it before, but I was starting to feel a little left out, to tell the truth."

"I thought screenplays were the LA Lotto."

"Naw. A good lotto is one you can win."

She favored him with half a smile and he saw that she had a lopsided, left-hand dimple.

"You're from LA, then?"

"Got it in one. Orange County. I'm a third-generation failed actor. Grandpa once had a line in a Hitchcock film. Mom was the ditzy neighbor on a three-episode Fox sitcom in the 90s. I'm still waiting for my moment in the sun. You live here?"

"For now. Since September. I'm from Toronto."

"Canadia! Goddamn snowbacks. What are you doing in London?"

His comm rang, giving him a moment to gather his cover story. "Hello?"

"Art! It's Fede!" Federico was another provocateur in GMT. He wasn't exactly Art's superior—the tribes didn't work like that—but he had seniority.

"Fede—can I call you back?"

"Look, I heard about your accident, and I wouldn't have called, but it's urgent."

Art groaned and rolled his eyes in Linda's direction to let her know that he, too, was exasperated by the call, then retreated to the other side of his bed and hunched over.

"What is it?"

"We've been sniffed. I'm four-fifths positive."

Art groaned again. Fede lived in perennial terror of being found out and exposed as an ESTribesman, fired, deported, humiliated. He was always at least three-fifths positive, and the extra fifth was hardly an anomaly. "What's up now?"

"It's the VP of HR at Virgin/Deutsche Telekom. He's called me in for a meeting this afternoon. Wants

31

to go over the core hours recommendation." Fede was a McKinsey consultant offline, producing inflammatory recommendation packages for Fortune 100 companies. He was working the lazy-Euro angle, pushing for extra daycare, time off for sick relatives and spouses. The last policy binder he'd dumped on V/DT had contained enough obscure leave-granting clauses that an employee who was sufficiently lawyer-minded could conceivably claim 450 days of paid leave a year. Now he was pushing for the abolishment of "core hours," Corporate Eurospeak for the time after lunch but before afternoon naps when everyone showed up at the office, so that they could get some face-time. Enough of this, and GMT would be the laughingstock of the world, and so caught up in internecine struggles that the clear superiority of the stress-feeding EST ethos would sweep them away. That was the theory, anyway. Of course, there were rival Tribalists in every single management consulting firm in the world working against us. Management consultants have always worked on old-boys' networks, after all—it was a very short step from interning your frat buddy to interning your Tribesman. If the Tribes did not exist, it would be necessary for McKinsey and its unindicted co-conspirators around the world to invent them.

"That's it? A meeting? Jesus, it's just a meeting. He probably wants you to reassure him before he presents to the CEO, is all."

"No, I'm sure that's not it. He's got us sniffed—both

of us. He's been going through the product-design stuff, too, which is totally outside of his bailiwick. I tried to call him yesterday and his voicemail rolled over to a boardroom in O'Malley House." O'Malley House was the usability lab, a nice old row of connected Victorian townhouses just off Piccadilly. It was where Art consulted out of. Also, two-hundred-odd usability specialists, product designers, experience engineers, cog-psych cranks and other tinkerers with the mind. They were the hairface hackers of Art's generation, unmanageable creative darlings—no surprise that the VP of HR would have cause to spend a little face-time with someone there. Try telling Fede that, though.

"All right, Fede, what do you want me to do?"

"Just— Just be careful. Sanitize your storage. I'm pushing a new personal key to you now, too. Hcrc, I'll read you the fingerprint." The key would be an unimaginably long string of crypto-gibberish, and just to make sure that it wasn't intercepted and changed en route, Fede wanted to read him a slightly less long mathematical fingerprint hashed out of it. Once it arrived, Art was supposed to generate a fingerprint from Fede's new key and compare it to the one that Fede wanted him to jot down.

Art closed his eyes and reclined. "All right, I've got a pen," he said, though he had no such thing.

Fede read him the long, long string of digits and characters and he repeated them back, pretending to be noting them down. Paranoid bastard.

"OK, I got it. I'll get you a new key later today, all right?"

"Do it quick, man."

"Whatever, Fede. Back off, OK?"

"Sorry, sorry. Oh, and feel better, all right?"

"Bye, Fede."

"What was *that*?" Linda had her neck craned around to watch him.

He slipped into his cover story with a conscious effort. "I'm a user-experience consultant. My coworkers are all paranoid about a deadline."

She rolled her eyes. "Not another one. God. Look, we go out for dinner, don't say a word about the kerb design or the waiter or the menu or the presentation, OK? OK? I'm serious."

Art solemnly crossed his heart. "Who else do you know in the biz?"

"My ex. He wouldn't or couldn't shut up about how much everything sucked. He was right, but so what? I wanted to enjoy it, suckitude and all."

"OK, I promise. We're going out for dinner, then?"

"The minute I can walk, you're taking me out for as much flesh and entrails as I can eat."

"It's a deal."

And then they both slept again.

Met cute, huh? Linda was short and curvy, dark eyes and pursed lips and an hourglass figure that she thought made her look topheavy and big-assed, but I thought she was fabulous and soft and bouncy. She tasted like pepper, and her hair smelled of the abstruse polymers that kept it hanging in a brusque bob that brushed her firm, long jawline.

I'm getting a sunburn, and the pebbles on the roof are digging into my ass. I don't know if I'm going to push the pencil or not, but if I do, it's going to be somewhere more comfortable than this roof.

Except that the roof door, which I had wedged open after I snuck away from my attendants and slunk up the firecode-mandated stairwell, is locked. The small cairn of pebbles that I created in front of it has been strewn apart. It is locked tight. And me without my comm. Ah, me. I take an inventory of my person: a pencil, a hospital gown, a pair of boxer shorts and a head full of bad cess. I am 450 feet above the summery, muggy, verdant Massachusetts countryside. It is very hot, and I am turning the color of the Barbie aisle at FAO Schwartz, a kind of labial pink that is both painful and perversely cheerful.

I've spent my life going in the back door and coming out the side door. That's the way it is now. When it only takes two years for your job to morph into something that would have been unimaginable twenty-four months before, it's not really practical to go in through the front door. Not really practical to get the degree, the certification, the appropriate experience. I mean, even if you went back to university, the major you'd need by the time you graduated would be in a subject that hadn't been invented when you enrolled. So I'm good at back doors and side doors. It's what the Tribe does for me—provides me with entries into places where I technically don't belong. And thank God for them, anyway. Without the Tribes, *no one* would be qualified to do *anything* worth doing.

Going out the side door has backfired on me today, though.

Oh. Shit. I peer over the building's edge, down into the parking lot. The cars are thinly spread, the weather too fine for anyone out there in the real world to be visiting with their crazy relatives. Half a dozen beaters are parked down there, methane-breathers that the ESTalists call fartmobiles. I'd been driving something much the same on that fateful Leap Forward day in London. I left something out of my inventory: pebbles. The roof is littered, covered with a layer of gray, round riverstones, about the size of wasabi chickpeas. No one down there is going to notice me all the way up here. Not without that I give them a sign. A cracked windshield or two ought to do it.

I gather a small pile of rocks by the roof's edge and carefully take aim. I have to be cautious. Careful. A pebble dropped from this height—I remember the stories about the penny dropped from the top of the CN Tower that sunk six inches into the concrete below.

I select a small piece of gravel and carefully aim for the windshield of a little blue Sony Veddic and it's bombs away. I can only follow the stone's progress for a few seconds before my eyes can no longer disambiguate it from the surrounding countryside. What little I do see of its trajectory is disheartening, though: the wind whips it away on an almost horizontal parabola, off towards Boston. Forgetting all about Newton, I try lobbing and then hurling the gravel downward, but it gets taken away, off to neverneverland, and the windscreens remain whole.

I go off to prospect for bigger rocks.

You know the sort of horror movie where the suspense builds and builds and builds, partially collapsed at regular intervals by something jumping out and yelling "Boo!" whereupon the heroes have to flee, deeper into danger, and the tension rises and rises? You know how sometimes the director just doesn't know when to quit, and the bogeymen keep jumping out and yelling Boo, the wobbly bridges keep on collapsing, the small arms fire keeps blowing out more windows in the office tower?

It's not like the tension goes away—it just gets boring. Boring tension. You know that the climax is coming soon, that any minute now Our Hero will face down the archvillain and either kick his ass or have his ass kicked, the whole world riding on the outcome. You know that it will be satisfying, with much explosions and partial nudity. You know that afterward, Our Hero will retire to the space-bar and chill out and collect kisses from the love interest and that we'll all have a moment to get our adrenals back under control before the hand pops out of the grave and we all give a nervous jump and start eagerly anticipating the sequel.

You just wish it would *happen* already. You just wish that the little climaces could be taken as read, that the director would trust the audience to know that Our Hero really does wade through an entire ocean of shit en route to the final showdown.

I'm bored with being excited. I've been betrayed, menaced, institutionalized and stranded on the roof of a nuthouse, and I just want the fucking climax to come by and happen to me, so that I can know: smart or happy.

I've found a half-brick that was being used to hold down the tar paper around an exhaust chimney. I should've used that to hold the door open, but it's way the hell the other side of the roof, and I'd been really pleased with my little pebbly doorstop. Besides, I'm starting to suspect that the doorjamb didn't fail; that it was sabotaged by some malevolently playful goon from the sanatorium. An object lesson or something.

I heft the brick. I release the brick. It falls, and falls, and falls, and hits the little blue fartmobile square on the trunk, punching a hole through the cheap aluminum lid.

And the fartmobile explodes. First there is a geyser of blue flame as the tank's puncture wound jets a stream of ignited assoline skyward, and then it blows back into the tank and *boom*, the fartmobile is in one billion shards, rising like a parachute in an updraft. I can feel the heat on my bare, sun-tender skin, even from this distance.

Explosions. Partial nudity. Somehow, though, I know that this isn't the climax.

>>>>>>>>>>8

Linda didn't like to argue—fight: yes, argue: no. That was going to be a problem, Art knew, but when you're falling in love, you're able to rationalize all kinds of things.

The yobs who cornered them on the way out of a bloody supper of contraband, antisocial animal flesh were young, large and bristling with testosterone. They wore killsport armor with strategic transparent panels that revealed their steroid-curdled muscles, visible through the likewise transparent insets they'd had grafted in place of the skin that covered their abs and quads. There were three of them, grinning and flexing, and they boxed in Art and Linda in the tiny, shuttered entrance of a Boots Pharmacy.

"Evening, sir, evening, miss," one said.

"Hey," Art muttered and looked over the yob's shoulder, trying to spot a secam or a cop. Neither was in sight.

"I wonder if we could beg a favor of you?" another said.

"Sure," Art said.

"You're American, aren't you?" the third said.

"Canadian, actually."

"Marvelous. Bloody marvelous. I hear that Canada's a lovely place. How are you enjoying England?"

"I live here, actually. I like it a lot."

"Glad to hear that, sir. And you, miss?"

Linda was wide-eyed, halfway behind Art. "It's fine."

"Good to hear," the first one said, grinning even more broadly. "Now, as to that favor. My friends and I, we've got a problem. We've grown bored of our wallets. They are dull and uninteresting."

"And empty," the third one interjected, with a little, stoned giggle.

"Oh yes, and empty. We thought, well, perhaps you visitors from abroad would find them suitable souvenirs of England. We thought perhaps you'd like to trade, like?"

Art smiled in spite of himself. He hadn't been mugged in London, but he'd heard of this. Ever since a pair of Manchester toughs had been acquitted based on the claim that their robbery and menacing of a Pakistani couple had been a simple cross-cultural misunderstanding, crafty British yobs had been taking off increasingly baroque scores from tourists.

Art felt the familiar buzz that meant he was about to get into an argument, and before he knew it, he was talking: "Do you really think that'd hold up in court? I think that even the dimmest judge would be able to tell that the idea of a Canadian being mistaken about trading two wallets full of cash for three empty ones was in no way an error in cross-cultural communication. Really now. If you're going to mug us—"

"Mug you, sir? Dear oh dear, who's mugging you?" the first one said.

"Well, in that case, you won't mind if we say no, right?"

"Well, it would be rather rude," the first said. "After all, we're offering you a souvenir in the spirit of transatlantic solidarity. Genuine English leather, mine is. Belonged to my grandfather."

"Let me see it," Art said.

"Beg pardon?"

"I want to see it. If we're going to trade, I should be able to examine the goods first, right?"

"All right, sir, all right, here you are."

The wallet was tattered and leather, and it was indeed made in England, as the frayed tag sewn into the billfold attested. Art turned it over in his hands, then, still smiling, emptied the card slot and started paging through the ID. "Lester?"

Lester swore under his breath. "Les, actually. Hand those over, please—they don't come with the wallet."

"They don't? But surely a real British wallet is hardly complete without real British identification. Maybe I could keep the NHS card, something to show around to Americans. They think socialized medicine is a fairy tale, you know."

"I really must insist, sir."

"Fuck it, Les," the second one said, reaching into his pocket. "This is stupid. Get the money, and let's push off."

"It's not that easy any more, is it?" the third one said. "Fellow's got your name, Les. 'Sbad."

"Well, yes, of course I do," Art said. "But so what? You three are hardly nondescript. You think it'd be hard to pick your faces out of a rogues gallery? Oh, and wait a minute! Isn't this a trade? What happened to the spirit of transatlantic solidarity?"

"Right," Les said. "Don't matter if you've got my name, 'cos we're all friends, right, sir?"

"Right!" Art said. He put the tattered wallet in his already bulging jacket pocket, making a great show of tamping it down so it wouldn't come loose. Once his hand was free, he extended it. "Art Berry. Late of Toronto. Pleased to meetcha!"

Les shook his hand. "I'm Les. These are my friends, Tony and Tom."

"Fuck!" Tom, the second one, said. "Les, you stupid cunt! Now they got our names, too!" The hand he'd put in his pocket came out, holding a tazer that sparked and hummed. "Gotta get rid of 'em now."

Art smiled, and reached very slowly into his pocket. He pulled out his comm, dislodging Les's wallet so that it fell to the street. Les, Tom and Tony stared at the glowing comm in his hand. "Could you repeat that, Tom? I don't think the 999 operator heard you clearly."

Tom stared dumbfounded at the comm, watching it as though it were a snake. The numbers "999" were clearly visible on its display, along with the position data that pinpointed its location to the meter. Les turned abruptly and began walking briskly towards the tube station. In a moment, Tony followed, leaving Tom alone, the tazer still hissing and spitting. His face contorted with frustrated anger, and he feinted with the tazer, barking a laugh when Art and Linda cringed back, then he took off at a good run after his mates.

Art clamped the comm to his head. "They've gone away," he announced, prideful. "Did you get that exchange? There were three of them and they've gone away."

From the comm came a tight, efficient voice, a male emergency operator. The speech was accented, and it took a moment to place it. Then Art remembered that the overnight emergency call-centers had been outsourced by the English government to low-cost cube-farms in Manila. "Yes, Mr. Berry." His comm

43

had already transmitted his name, immigration status and location, creating a degree of customization more typical of fast-food delivery than governmental bureaucracies. That was bad, Art thought, professionally. GMT polezeidom was meant to be a solid wall of oatmeal-thick bureaucracy, courtesy of some crafty, anonymous PDTalist. "Please, stay at your current location. The police will be on the scene shortly. Very well done, sir."

Art turned to Linda, triumphant, ready for the traditional, postrhetorical accolades that witnesses of his verbal acrobatics were wont to dole out, and found her in an attitude of abject terror. Her eyes were crazily wide, the whites visible around the irises—something he'd read about but never seen firsthand. She was breathing shallowly and had gone ashen.

Though they were not an actual couple yet, Art tried to gather her into his arms for some manly comforting, but she was stiff in his embrace, and after a moment, planted her palms on his chest and pushed him back firmly, even aggressively.

"Are you all right?" he asked. He was adrenalized, flushed.

"*What if they'd decided to kill us?*" she said, spittle flying from her lips.

"Oh, they weren't going to hurt us," he said. "No guts at all."

"God*dammit*, you didn't know that! Where do you get off playing around with *my* safety? Why the hell didn't you just hand over your wallet, call the cops and be done with it? Macho fucking horseshit!"

The triumph was fading, fast replaced by anger. "What's wrong with you? Do you always have to snatch defeat from the jaws of victory? I just beat off those three assholes without raising a hand, and all you want to do is criticize? Christ, OK, next time we can hand over our wallets. Maybe they'll want a little rape, too—should I go along with that? You just tell me what the rules are, and I'll be sure and obey them."

"You fucking *pig*! Where the fuck do you get off raising your voice to me? And don't you *ever* joke about rape. It's not even slightly funny, you arrogant fucking prick."

Art's triumph deflated. "Jesus," he said, "Jesus, Linda, I'm sorry. I didn't realize how scared you must have been—"

"You don't know what you're talking about. I've been mugged a dozen times. I hand over my wallet, cancel my cards, go to my insurer. No one's ever hurt me. I wasn't the least bit scared until you opened up your big goddamned mouth."

"Sorry, sorry. Sorry about the rape crack. I was just trying to make a point. I didn't know—" He wanted to say, *I didn't know you'd been raped*, but thought better of it. "—it was so . . . *personal* for you—"

"Oh, Christ. Just because I don't want to joke about rape, you think I'm some kind of *victim*, that *I've* been raped"—Art grimaced—"well, I haven't, shit-head. But it's not something you should be using as a goddamned example in one of your stupid points. Rape is serious."

The cops arrived then, two of them on scooters, looking like meter maids. Art and Linda glared at each other for a moment, then forced smiles at the cops, who had dismounted and shed their helmets. They were young men, in their twenties, and to Art they looked like kids playing dress up.

"Evening sir, miss," one said. "I'm PC McGivens and this is PC DeMoss. You called emergency services?" McGivens had his comm out and it was pointed at them, slurping in their identity on police override.

"Yes," Art said. "But it's OK now. They took off. One of them left his wallet behind." He bent and picked it up and made to hand it to PC DeMoss, who was closer. The cop ignored it.

"Please sir, put that down. We'll gather the evidence."

Art lowered it to the ground, felt himself blushing. His hands were shaking now, whether from embarrassment, triumph or hurt he couldn't say. He held up his now-empty palms in a gesture of surrender.

"Step over here, please, sir," PC McGivens said, and led him off a short ways, while PC DeMoss closed on Linda.

"Now, sir," McGivens said, in a businesslike way, "please tell me exactly what happened."

So Art did, tastefully omitting the meat-parlor where the evening's festivities had begun. He started to get into it, to evangelize his fast-thinking bravery with the phone. McGivens obliged him with a little grin.

"Very good. Now, again, please, sir?"

"I'm sorry?" Art said.

"Can you repeat it, please? Procedure."

"Why?"

"Can't really say, sir. It's procedure."

Art thought about arguing, but managed to control the impulse. The man was a cop, he was a foreigner— albeit a thoroughly documented one—and what would it cost? He'd probably left something out anyway.

He retold the story from the top, speaking slowly and clearly. PC McGivens aimed his comm Artwards, and tapped out the occasional note as Art spoke.

"Thank you, sir. Now, once more, please?"

Art blew out an exasperated sigh. His feet hurt, and his bladder was swollen with drink. "You're joking."

"No sir, I'm afraid not. Procedure."

"But it's stupid! The guys who tried to mug us are long gone, I've given you their descriptions, you have their *identification*—" But they didn't, not yet. The wallet still lay where Art had dropped it.

PC McGivens shook his head slowly, as though marveling at the previously unsuspected inanity of his daily round. "All very true, sir, but it's procedure. Worked out by some clever lad using statistics.

47

All this, it increases our success rate. 'Sproven."

Here it was. Some busy tribalist provocateur, some compatriot of Fede, had stirred the oats into Her Majesty's Royal Constabulary. Art snuck a look at Linda, who was no doubt being subjected to the same procedure by PC DeMoss. She'd lost her rigid, angry posture, and was seemingly—amazingly—enjoying herself, chatting up the constable like an old pal.

"How many more times have we got to do this, officer?"

"This is the last time you'll have to repeat it to me."

Art's professional instincts perked up at the weasel words in the sentence. "To you? Who else do I need to go over this with?"

The officer shook his head, caught out. "Well, you'll have to repeat it three times to PC DeMoss, once he's done with your friend, sir. Procedure."

"How about this," Art says, "how about I record this last statement to you with my comm, and then I can *play it back* three times for PC DeMoss?"

"Oh, I'm sure that won't do, sir. Not really the spirit of the thing, is it?"

"And what *is* the spirit of the thing? Humiliation? Boredom? An exercise in raw power?"

PC McGivens lost his faint smile. "I really couldn't say, sir. Now, again if you please?"

"What if I don't please? I haven't been assaulted. I haven't been robbed. It's none of my business. What if I walk away right now?"

"Not really allowed, sir. It's expected that everyone in England—HM's subjects *and her guests*—will assist the police with their inquiries. Required, actually."

Reminded of his precarious immigration status, Art lost his attitude. "Once more for you, three more times for your partner, and we're done, right? I want to get home."

"We'll see, sir."

Art recited the facts a third time, and they waited while Linda finished her third recounting.

He switched over to PC DeMoss, who pointed his comm expectantly. "Is all this just to make people reluctant to call the cops? I mean, this whole procedure seems like a hell of a disincentive."

"Just the way we do things, sir," PC DeMoss said without rancor. "Now, let's have it, if you please?"

From a few yards away, Linda laughed at something PC McGivens said, which just escalated Art's frustration. He spat out the description three times fast. "Now, I need to find a toilet. Are we done yet?"

" 'Fraid not, sir. Going to have to come by the Station House to look through some photos. There's a toilet there."

"It can't wait that long, officer."

PC DeMoss gave him a reproachful look.

"I'm sorry, all right?" Art said. "I lack the foresight to empty my bladder before being accosted in the street. That being said, can we arrive at some kind of solution?" In his head, Art was already writing an angry letter to the *Times*, dripping with sarcasm.

"Just a moment, sir," PC DeMoss said. He conferred briefly with his partner, leaving Art to stare ruefully at their backs and avoid Linda's gaze. When he finally met it, she gave him a sunny smile. It seemed that she—at least—wasn't angry anymore.

"OK, Darrell, I'll meet you back here," PC McGivens said.

"Come this way, please, sir," PC DeMoss said, striking off for the High Street. "There's a pub 'round the corner where you can use the facilities."

>>>>>>>>>>>9

It was nearly dawn before they finally made their way out of the police station and back into the street. After identifying Les from an online rogues' gallery, Art had spent the next six hours sitting on a hard bench, chording desultorily on his thigh, doing some housekeeping.

This business of being an agent-provocateur was complicated in the extreme, though it had sounded like a good idea when he was living in San Francisco and hating every inch of the city, from the alleged pizza to the fucking! drivers!—in New York, the theory went, drivers used their horns by way of shouting "Olé!" as in, "Olé! You changed lanes!" "Olé! You cut me off!" "Olé! You're driving on the sidewalk!" while in San Francisco, a honking horn meant, "I wish you were dead. Have a nice day. Dude."

And the body language was all screwed up out west. Art believed that your entire unconscious affect was determined by your upbringing. You learned how to stand, how to hold your face in repose, how to gesture, from the adults around you while you were growing up. The Pacific Standard Tribe always seemed a little bovine to him, their facial muscles long conditioned to relax into a kind of spacey, gullible senescence.

Beauty, too. Your local definition of attractive and ugly was conditioned by the people around you at puberty. There was a Pacific "look" that was indefinably off. Hard to say what it was, just that when he went out to a bar or got stuck on a crowded train, the girls just didn't seem all that attractive to him. Objectively, he could recognize their prettiness, but it didn't stir him the way the girls cruising the Chelsea Antiques Market or lounging around Harvard Square could.

He'd always felt at a slight angle to reality in California, something that was reinforced by his continuous efforts in the Tribe, from chatting and gaming until the sun rose, dragging his caffeine-deficient ass around to his clients in a kind of fog before going home, catching a nap and hopping back online at 3 or 4 when the high-octane NYC early risers were practicing work-avoidance and clattering around with their comms.

Gradually, he penetrated deeper into the Tribe, getting invites into private channels, intimate environments where he found himself spilling the most private details of his life. The Tribe stuck together, finding work for each other, offering advice, and it was only a matter of time before someone offered him a gig.

That was Fede, who practically invented Tribal agent-provocateurs. He'd been working for McKinsey, systematically undermining their GMT-based clients with plausibly terrible advice, creating Achilles' heels that their East Coast competitors could exploit. The entire European trust-architecture for relay networks had been ceded by Virgin/Deutsche Telekom to a scrappy band of AT&T Labs refugees whose New Jersey headquarters hosted all the cellular reputation data that Euros' comms consulted when they were routing their calls. The Jersey clients had funneled a nice chunk of the proceeds to Fede's account in the form of rigged winnings from an offshore casino that the Tribe used to launder its money.

Now V/DT was striking back, angling for a government contract in Massachusetts, a fat bit of pork for managing payments to rightsholders whose media was assessed at the MassPike's tollbooths. Rights-societies were a fabulous opportunity to skim and launder and spindle money in plenty, and Virgin's massive repertoire combined with Deutsche Telekom's Teutonic attention to detail was a tough combination to beat. Needless to say, the Route 128–based Tribalists who had the existing contract needed an edge, and would pay handsomely for it.

London nights seemed like a step up from San Francisco mornings to Art—instead of getting up at 4AM to get NYC, he could sleep in and chat them up through the night. The Euro sensibility, with its many nap-breaks, statutory holidays and extended vacations seemed ideally suited to a double agent's life.

But Art hadn't counted on the Tribalists' hands-on approach to his work. They obsessively grepped his daily feed of spreadsheets, whiteboard-output, memos and conversation reports for any of ten thousand hot keywords, querying him for deeper detail on trivial, half-remembered bullshit sessions with the V/DT's user-experience engineers. His comm buzzed and blipped at all hours, and his payoff was dependent on his prompt response. They were running him ragged.

Four hours in the police station gave Art ample opportunity to catch up on the backlog of finicky queries. Since the accident, he'd been distracted and tardy, and had begun to invent his responses, since it all seemed so trivial to him anyway.

Fede had sent him about a thousand nagging notes reminding him to generate a new key and phone with the fingerprint. Christ. Fede had been with McKinsey for most of his adult life, and he was superparanoid about being exposed and disgraced in their ranks. Art's experience with the other McKinsey people around the office suggested that the notion of any of those overpaid buzzword-slingers sniffing their traffic was about as likely as a lightning strike. Heaving a dramatic sigh for his own benefit, he began the lengthy process of generating enough randomness to seed the key, mashing the keyboard, whispering nonsense syllables, and pointing the comm's camera lens at arbitrary corners of the police station. After ten minutes of crypto-Tourette's, the comm announced that he'd been sufficiently random and prompted him for a passphrase. Jesus. What a pain in the ass. He struggled to recall all the words to the theme song from a CBC sitcom he'd watched as a kid, and then his comm went into a full-on churn as it laboriously re-ciphered all of his stored files with the new key, leaving Art to login while he waited.

Trepan: Afternoon!

Colonelonic: Hey, Trepan. How's it going?

Trepan: Foul. I'm stuck at a copshop in London with my
    thumb up my ass. I got mugged.

Colonelonic: Yikes! You OK?

Ballgravy: Shit!

Trepan: Oh, I'm fine——just bored. They didn't hurt me. I
    commed 999 while they were running their game and
    showed it to them when they got ready to do the deed,
    so they took off.

##Colonelonic laughs

Ballgravy: Britain==ass. Lon-dong.

Colonelonic: Sweet!

Trepan: Thanks. Now if the cops would only finish the paper-
    work . . .

Colonelonic: What are you doing in London, anyway?

Ballgravy: Ass ass ass

Colonelonic: Shut up, Bgravy

Ballgravy: Blow me

Trepan: What's wrong with you, Ballgravy? We're having a
    grown-up conversation here

Ballgravy: Just don't like Brits.

Trepan: What, all of them?

Ballgravy: Whatever——all the ones I've met have been
    tight-ass pricks

##Colonelonic: (private) He's just a troll, ignore him

/private Colonelonic: Watch this

Trepan: How many?

Ballgravy: How many what?

Trepan: Have you met?

Ballgravy: Enough

Trepan: > 100?

Ballgravy: No

Trepan: > 50?

Ballgravy: No

Trepan: > 10?

Ballgravy: Around 10

Trepan: Where are you from?

Ballgravy: Queens

Trepan: Well, you're not going to believe this, but you're
    the tenth person from Queens I've met——and you're
    all morons who pick fights with strangers in chat-
    rooms

Colonelonic: Queens==ass

Trepan: Ass ass ass

Ballgravy: Fuck you both

##Ballgravy has left channel #EST.chatter

Colonelonic: Nicely done

Colonelonic: He's been boring me stupid for the past hour, following me from channel to channel

Colonelonic: What are you doing in London, anyway?

Trepan: Like I said, waiting for the cops

Colonelonic: But why are you there in the first place

Trepan: /private Colonelonic It's a work thing. For EST.

##Colonelonic: (private) No shit?

Trepan: /private Colonelonic Yeah. Can't really say much more, you understand

##Colonelonic: (private) Cool! Any more jobs? One more day at Merrill-Lynch and I'm gonna kill someone

Trepan: /private Colonelonic Sorry, no. There must be some perks though.

##Colonelonic: (private) I can pick fights with strangers in chat rooms! Also, I get to play with Lexis-Nexis all I want

Trepan: /private Colonelonic That's pretty rad, anyway

##Ballgravy has joined channel #EST.chatter

Ballgravy: Homos

Trepan: Oh Christ, are you back again, Queens?

Colonelonic: I've gotta go anyway

Trepan: See ya

##Colonelonic has left channel #EST.chatter

##Trepan has left channel #EST.chatter

Art stood up and blinked. He approached the desk sergeant and asked if he thought it would be much longer. The sergeant fiddled with a comm for a moment, then said, "Oh, we're quite done with you sir, thank you." Art repressed a vituperative response, counted three, then thanked the cop.

He commed Linda.

"What's up?"

"They say we're free to go. I think they've been just keeping us here for shits and giggles. Can you believe that?"

"Whatever—I've been having a nice chat with Constable McGivens. Constable, is it all right if we go now?"

There was some distant, English rumbling, then Linda giggled. "All right, then. Thank you so much, officer!

"Art? I'll meet you at the front doors, all right?"

"That's great," Art said. He stretched. His ass was numb, his head throbbed, and he wanted to strangle Linda.

She emerged into the dawn blinking and grinning, and surprised him with a long, full-body hug. "Sorry I was so snappish before," she said. "I was just scared. The cops say that you were quite brave. Thank you."

Art's adrenals dry-fired as he tried to work up a good angry head of steam, then he gave up. "It's all right."

"Let's go get some breakfast, OK?"

The parking lot is aswarm with people, fire engines and ambulances. There's a siren going off somewhere down in the bowels of the sanatorium, and still I can't get anyone to look up at the goddamned roof.

I've tried hollering myself hoarse into the updrafts from the cheery blaze, but the wind's against me, my shouts rising up past my ears. I've tried dropping more pebbles, but the winds whip them away, and I've learned my lesson about half-bricks.

Weirdly, I'm not worried about getting into trouble. I've already been involuntarily committed by the Tribe's enemies, the massed and devious forces of the Pacific Daylight Tribe and the Greenwich Mean Tribe. I am officially Not Responsible. Confused and Prone to Wandering. Coo-Coo for Coco-Puffs. It's not like I hurt anyone, just decremented the number of road-worthy fartmobiles by one.

I got up this morning at four, awakened by the tiniest sound from the ward corridors, a wheel from a pharmaceuticals tray maybe. Three weeks on medically prescribed sleepytime drugs have barely scratched the surface of the damage wrought by years of circadian abuse. I'd been having a fragile shadow of a dream, the ghost of a REM cycle, and it was the old dream, the dream of the doctor's office and the older kids who could manage the trick of making a picture into reality.

I went from that state to total wakefulness in an instant, and knew to a certainty that I wouldn't be sleeping again any time soon. I paced my small room, smelled the cheerful flowers my cousins brought last week when they visited from Toronto, watched the horizon for signs of a breaking dawn. I wished futilely for my comm and a nice private channel where I could sling some bullshit and have some slung in my direction, just connect with another human being at a nice, safe remove.

They chide me for arguing on the ward, call it belligerence and try to sidetrack me with questions about my motivations, a tactic rating barely above ad hominems in my book. No one to talk to—the other patients get violent or nod off, depending on their medication levels, and the staff just patronize me.

Four AM and I'm going nuts, hamsters in my mind spinning their wheels at a thousand RPM, chittering away. I snort—if I wasn't crazy to begin with, I'm sure getting there.

The hamsters won't stop arguing with each other over all the terrible errors of judgment I've made to get here. Trusting the Tribe, trusting strangers. Argue, argue, argue. God, if only someone else were around, I could argue the definition of sanity, I could argue the ethics of involuntary committal, I could argue the food. But my head is full of argument and there's nowhere to spill it and soon enough I'll be talking aloud, arguing with the air like the schizoids on the ward who muttergrumbleshout through the day and through the night.

Why didn't I just leave London when I could, come home, move in with Gran, get a regular job? Why didn't I swear off the whole business of secrecy and provocation?

I was too smart for my own good. I could always argue myself into doing the sexy, futuristic thing instead of being a nice, mundane, nonaffiliated individual. Too smart to settle down, take a job and watch TV after work, spend two weeks a year at the cottage and go online to find movie listings. Too smart is too restless and no happiness, ever, without that it's chased by obsessive, maundering moping about what comes next.

Smart or happy?

The hamsters have hopped off their wheels and are gnawing at the blood-brain barrier, trying to get out of my skull. This is a good sanatorium, but still, the toilets are communal on my floor, which means that I've got an unlocked door that lights up at the nurses' station down the corridor when I open the door, and goes berserk if I don't reopen it again within the mandated fifteen-minute maximum potty-break. I figured out how to defeat the system the first day, but it was a theoretical hack, and now it's time to put it into practice.

I step out the door and the lintel goes pink, deepens

towards red. Once it's red, *whoopwhoopwhoop*. I pad down to the lav, step inside, wait, step out again. I go back to my room—the lintel is orange now—and open it, move my torso across the long electric eye, then pull it back and let the door swing closed. The lintel is white, and that means that the room thinks I'm inside, but I'm outside. You put your torso in, you take your torso out, you do the hokey-pokey and you shake it all about.

In the corridor. I pad away from the nurses' station, past the closed doors and through the muffled, narcotized groans and snores and farts that are the twilight symphony of night on the ward. I duck past an intersection, head for the elevator doors, then remember the tattletale I'm wearing on my ankle, which will go spectacularly berserk if I try to leave by that exit. Also, I'm in my underwear. I can't just walk nonchalantly into the lobby.

The ward is making wakeful sounds, and I'm sure I hear the soft tread of a white-soled shoe coming round the bend. I double my pace, begin to jog at random—the hamsters, they tell me I'm acting with all the forethought of a crazy person, and why not just report for extra meds instead of all this *mishegas*?

There's definitely someone coming down a nearby corridor. The tread of sneakers, the squeak of a wheel. I've seen what they do to the wanderers: a nice chemical straightjacket, a cocktail of pills that'll quiet the hamsters down for days. Time to get gone.

There's an EXIT sign glowing over a door at the far

end of the corridor. I pant towards it, find it propped open and the alarm system disabled by means of a strip of surgical tape. Stepping through into the emergency stairwell, I see an ashtray fashioned from a wadded up bit of tinfoil, heaped with butts—evidence of late-night smoke breaks by someone on the ward staff. Massachusetts's harsh antismoking regs are the best friend an escaping loony ever had.

The stairwell is gray and industrial and refreshingly hard-edged after three padded weeks on the ward. Down, down is the exit and freedom. Find clothes somewhere and out I go into Boston.

From below, then: the huffing, laborious breathing of some goddamned overweight, middle-aged doc climbing the stairs for his health. I peer down the well and see his gleaming pate, his white knuckles on the railing, two, maybe three flights down.

Up! Up to the roof. I'm on the twentieth floor, which means that I've got twenty-five more to go, two flights per, fifty in total, gotta move. Up! I stop two or three times and pant and wheeze and make it ten stories and collapse. I'm sweating freely—no air-conditioning in the stairwell, nor is there anything to mop up the sweat rolling down my body, filling the crack of my ass, coursing down my legs. I press my face to the cool painted cinderblock walls, one cheek and then the other, and continue on.

When I finally open the door that leads out onto the pebbled roof, the dawn cool is balm. Fingers of light are hauling the sunrise up over the horizon. I step onto the roof and feel the pebbles dig into the soft soles of my feet, cool as the bottom of the riverbed whence they'd been dredged. The door starts to swing shut heavily behind me, and I whirl and catch it just in time, getting my fingers mashed against the jamb for my trouble. I haul it back open again against its pneumatic closure mechanism.

Using the side of my foot as a bulldozer, I scrape up a cairn of pebbles as high as the door's bottom edge, twice as high. I fall into the rhythm of the work, making the cairn higher and wider until I can't close the door no matter how I push against it. The last thing I want is to get stuck on the goddamn roof.

There's detritus mixed in with the pebbles: cigarette butts, burnt out matches, a condom wrapper and a bright yellow Eberhard pencil with a point as sharp as a spear, the eraser as pink and softly resilient as a nipple.

I pick up the pencil and twiddle it between forefinger and thumb, tap a nervous rattle against the roof's edge as I dangle my feet over the bottomless plummet until the sun is high and warm on my skin.

The hamsters get going again once the sun is high and the cars start pulling into the parking lot below, rattling and chittering and whispering, yes o yes, put the pencil in your nose, wouldn't you rather be happy than smart?

Art and Linda in Linda's minuscule joke of a flat. She's two months into a six-month house-swap with some friends of friends who have a fourth-storey walkup in Kensington with a partial (i.e. fictional) view of the park. The lights are on timers and you need to race them to her flat's door, otherwise there's no way you'll fit the archaic key into the battered keyhole—the windows in the stairwell are so grimed as to provide more of a suggestion of light than light itself.

Art's ass aches and he paces the flat's three wee rooms and drinks hormone-enhanced high-energy liquid breakfast from the half-fridge in the efficiency kitchen. Linda's taken dibs on the first shower, which is fine by Art, who can't get the hang of the goddamned-English-plumbing, which delivers an energy-efficient, eat-your-vegetables-and-save-the-planet trickle of scalding water.

Art has switched off his comm, his frazzled nerves no longer capable of coping with its perennial and demanding beeping and buzzing. This is very nearly unthinkable but necessary, he rationalizes, given the extraordinary events of the past twenty-four hours. And Fede can go fuck himself, for that matter, that paranoid asshole, and then he can fuck the clients in Jersey and the whole of V/DT while he's at it.

The energy bev is kicking in and making his heart race and his pulse throb in his throat and he's so unbearably hyperkinetic that he turns the coffee table on its end in the galley kitchen and clears a space in the living room that's barely big enough to spin around in, and starts to work through a slow, slow set of Tai Chi, so slow that he barely moves at all, except that inside he can feel the moving, can feel the muscles' every flex and groan as they wind up release, move and swing and slide.

Single whip slides into crane opens wings and he needs to crouch down low, lower than his woolen slacks will let him, and they're grimy and gross anyway, so he undoes his belt and kicks them off. Down low as white crane opens wings and brush knee, punch, apparent closure, then low again, creakingly achingly low into wave hands like clouds, until his spine and his coccyx crackle and give, springing open, fascia open ribs open smooth breath rising and falling with his diaphragm mind smooth and sweat cool in the mat of his hair.

He moves through the set and does not notice Linda until he unwinds into a slow, ponderous lotus kick, closes again, breathes a moment and looks around slowly, grinning like a holy fool.

She's in a tartan housecoat with a threadbare towel wrapped around her hair, water beading on her bony ankles and long, skinny feet. "Art! God*damn*, Art! What the hell was that?"

"Tai Chi," he says, drawing a deep breath in through his nostrils, feeling each rib expand in turn, exhaling through his mouth. "I do it to unwind."

"It was beautiful! Art! Art. Art. That was, I mean, wow. Inspiring. Something. You're going to show me how to do that, Art. Right? You're gonna."

"I could try," Art says. "I'm not really qualified to teach it—I stopped going to class ten years ago."

"Shut, shut up, Art. You can teach that, damn, you can teach that, I know you can. That was, wow." She rushes forward and takes his hands. She squeezes and looks into his eyes. She squeezes again and tugs his hands towards her hips, reeling his chest towards her breasts tilting her chin up and angling that long jawline that's so long as to be almost horsey, but it isn't, it's strong and clean. Art smells shampoo and sandalwood talc and his skin puckers in a crinkle that's so sudden and massive that it's almost audible.

They've been together continuously for the past five days, almost without interruption and he's already conditioned to her smell and her body language and the subtle signals of her face's many mobile bits and pieces. She is afire, he is afire, their bodies are talking to each other in some secret language of shifting centers of gravity and unconscious pheromones, and his face tilts down towards her, slowly with all the time in the world. Lowers and lowers, week-old whiskers actually tickling the tip of her nose, his lips parting now, and her breath moistens them, beads them with liquid condensed out of her vapor.

His top lip touches her bottom lip. He could leave it at that and be happy, the touch is so satisfying, and he is contented there for a long moment, then moves to engage his lower lip, moving, tilting.

His comm rings.

His comm, which he has switched off, rings.

Shit.

"Hello!" he says, he shouts.

"Arthur?" says a voice that is old and hurt and melancholy. His Gran's voice. His Gran, who can override his ringer, switch on his comm at a distance because Art is a good grandson who was raised almost entirely by his saintly and frail (and depressive and melodramatic and obsessive) grandmother, and of course his comm is set to pass her calls. Not because he is a suck, but because he is loyal and sensitive and he loves his Gran.

"Gran, hi! Sorry, I was just in the middle of something, sorry." He checks his comm, which tells him that it's only six in the morning in Toronto, noon in London, and that the date is April 28, and that today is the day that he should have known his grandmother would call.

"You forgot," she says, no accusation, just a weary and disappointed sadness. He has indeed forgotten.

"No, Gran, I didn't forget."

But he did. It is the twenty-eighth of April, 2022, which means that it is twenty-one years to the day since his mother died. And he has forgotten.

"It's all right. You're busy, I understand. Tell me,

Art, how are you? When will you visit Toronto?"

"I'm fine, Gran. I'm sorry I haven't called, I've been sick." Shit. Wrong lie.

"You're sick? What's wrong?"

"It's nothing. I—I put my back out. Working too hard. Stress. It's nothing, Gran."

He chances to look up at Linda, who is standing where he left her when he dived reflexively for his comm, staring disbelievingly at him. Her robe is open to her navel, and he sees the three curls of pubic hair above the knot in its belt that curl towards her groin, sees the hourglass made by the edges of her breasts that are visible in the vee of the robe, sees the edge of one aureole, the left one. He is in a tee shirt and bare feet and boxers, crouching over his trousers, talking to his Gran, and he locks eyes with Linda and shakes his head apologetically, then settles down to sit cross-legged, hunched over an erection he didn't know he had, resolves to look at her while he talks.

"Stress! Always stress. You should take some vacation time. Are you seeing someone? A chiropractor?"

He's entangled in the lie. "Yes. I have an appointment tomorrow."

"How will you get there? Don't take the subway. Take a taxi. And give me the doctor's name, I'll look him up."

"I'll take a cab, it'll be fine, he's the only one my travel insurance covers."

"The only one? Art! What kind of insurance do you

have? I'll call them, I'll find you a chiropractor. Betty Melville, she has family in London, they'll know someone."

God. "It's fine, Gran. How are you?"

A sigh. "How am I? On this day, how am I?"

"How is your health? Are you keeping busy?"

"My health is fine. I keep busy. Father Ferlenghetti came to dinner last night at the house. I made a nice roast, and I'll have sandwiches today."

"That's good."

"I'm thinking of your mother, you know."

"I know."

"Do you think of her, Art? You were so young when she went, but you remember her, don't you?"

"I do, Gran." He remembers her, albeit dimly. He was barely nine when she died.

"Of course—of course you remember your mother. It's a terrible thing for a mother to live longer than her daughter."

His Gran says this every year. Art still hasn't figured out how to respond to it. Time for another stab at it. "I'm glad you're still here, Gran."

Wrong thing. Gran is sobbing now. Art drops his eyes from Linda's and looks at the crazy weft and woof of the faded old Oriental rug. "Oh, Gran," he says. "I'm sorry."

In truth, Art has mourned and buried his mother. He was raised just fine by his Gran, and when he remembers his mother, he is more sad about not being sad than sad about her.

"I'm an old lady, you know that. You'll remember me when I go, won't you Art?"

This, too, is a ritual question that Art can't answer well enough no matter how he practices. "Of course, Gran. But you'll be around for a good while yet!"

"When are you coming back to Toronto?" He'd ducked the question before, but Gran's a master of circling back and upping the ante. *Now that we've established my imminent demise . . .*

"Soon as I can, Gran. Maybe when I finish this contract. September, maybe."

"You'll stay here? I can take the sofa. When do you think you'll arrive? My friends all want to see you again. You remember Mrs. Tomkins? You used to play with her daughter Alice. Alice is single, you know. She has a good job, too—working at an insurance company. Maybe she can get you a better health plan."

"I don't know, Gran. I'll *try* to come back after I finish my contract, but I can't tell what'll be happening then. I'll let you know, OK?"

"Oh, Art. Please come back soon—I miss you. I'm going to visit your mother's grave today and put some flowers on it. They keep it very nice at Mount Pleasant, and the trees are just blooming now."

"I'll come back as soon as I can, Gran. I love you."

"I love you too, Arthur."

"Bye, Gran."

"I'll call you once I speak to Betty about the chiropractor, all right?"

"All right, Gran." He is going to have to go to the

chiropractor now, even though his back feels as good as it has in years. His Gran will be checking up on it.

"Bye, Arthur. I love you."

"Bye, Gran."

"Bye."

He shakes his head and holsters the comm back in his pants, then rocks back and lies down on the rug, facing the ceiling, eyes closed. A moment later, the hem of Linda's robe brushes his arm and she lies down next to him, takes his hand.

"Everything OK?"

"It's just my Gran." And he tells her about this date's significance.

"How did she die?"

"It was stupid. She slipped in the tub and cracked her skull on the tap. I was off at a friend's place for the weekend and no one found her for two days. She lived for a week on life support, and they pulled the plug. No brain activity. They wouldn't let me into the hospital room after the first day. My Gran practically moved in, though. She raised me after that. I think that if she hadn't had to take care of me, she would have just given up, you know? She's pretty lonely back home alone."

"What about your dad?"

"You know, there used to be a big mystery about that. Gran and Mom, they were always tragic and secretive when I asked them about him. I had lots of stories to explain his absence: ran off with another woman, thrown in jail for running guns, murdered in

71

a bar fight. I used to be a bit of a celeb at school—lots of kids didn't have dads around, but they all knew where their fathers were. We could always kill an afternoon making up his who and where and why. Even the teachers got into it, getting all apologetic when we had to do a genealogy project. I found out the truth, finally, when I was nineteen. Just looked it up online. It never occurred to me that my mom would be that secretive about something that was so easy to find out, so I never bothered."

"So, what happened to him?"

"Oh, you know. He and mom split when I was a kid. He moved back in with his folks in a little town in the Thousand Islands, near Ottawa. Four or five years later, he got a job planting trees for a summer up north, and he drowned swimming in a lake during a party. By the time I found out about him, his folks were dead, too."

"Did you tell your friends about him, once you found out?"

"Oh, by then I'd lost touch with most of them. After elementary school, we moved across town, to a condo my grandmother retired into on the lakeshore, out in the suburbs. In high school, I didn't really chum around much, so there wasn't anyone to talk to. I did tell my Gran though, asked her why it was such a big secret, and she said it wasn't, she said she'd told me years before, but she hadn't. I think that she and Mom just decided to wait until I was older before telling me, and then after my mom died, she just forgot that she hadn't told me. We got into a big fight over that."

"That's a weird story, dude. So, do you think of yourself as an orphan?"

Art rolls over on his side, face inches from hers, and snorts a laugh. "God, that's so—*Dickensian*. No one ever asked me that before. I don't think so. You can't really be an adult and be an orphan—you're just someone with dead parents. And I didn't find out about my dad until I was older, so I always figured that he was alive and well somewhere. What about your folks?"

Linda rolls over on her side, too, her robe slipping off her lower breast. Art is aroused by it, but not crazily so—somewhere in telling his story, he's figured out that sex is a foregone conclusion, and now they're just getting through some nice foreplay. He smiles down at her nipple, which is brown as a bar of Belgian chocolate, aureole the size of a round of individual cheese and nipple itself a surprisingly chunky square of crinkled flesh. She follows his eyes and smiles at him, then puts his hand over her breast, covers it with hers.

"I told you about my mom, right? Wanted to act— who doesn't? But she was too conscious of the cliché to mope about it. She got some little parts—nothing fab, then went on to work at a Sony dealership. Ten years later, she bought a franchise. Dad and second-wife run a retreat in West Hollywood for sexually dysfunctional couples. No sibs. Happy childhood.

Happy adolescence. Largely unsatisfying adulthood, to date."

"Wow, you sound like you've practiced that."

She tweaks his nose, then drapes her arm across his chest. "Got me. Always writing my autobiography in my head—gotta have a snappy opener when I'm cornered by the stalkerazzi."

He laces his fingers in hers, moves close enough to smell her toothpaste-sweet breath. "Tell me something unrehearsed about growing up."

"That's a stupid request." Her tone is snappish, and her fingers stiffen in his.

"Why?"

"It just is! Don't try to get under my skin, OK? My childhood was fine."

"Look, I don't want to piss you off. I'm just trying to get to know you. Because . . . you know . . . I like you. A lot. And I try to get to know the people I like."

She smiles her lopsided dimple. "Sorry, I just don't like people who try to mess with my head. My problem, not yours. OK, something unrehearsed." She closes her eyes and treats him to the smooth pinkness of her eyelids, and keeps them closed as she speaks. "I once stole a Veddic Series 7 off my mom's lot, when I was fifteen. It had all the girly safety features, including a tracker and a panic button, but I didn't think my mom would miss it. I just wanted to take it out for a drive. It's LA, right? No wheels, no life. So I get as far as Venice Beach, and I'm cruising the Boardwalk—this was just after it went topless, so I was swinging in

74

the breeze—and suddenly the engine dies, right in the middle of this clump of out-of-towners, frat kids from Kansas or something. Mom had called in a dealer override and Sony shut down the engine by radio."

"Wow, what did you do?"

"Well, I put my shirt back on. Then I popped the hood and poked randomly at the engine, pulling out the user-servicables and rescating them. The thing was newer than new, right? How could it be broken already? The fratboys all gathered around and gave me advice, and I played up all bitchy, you know, 'I've been fixing these things since I was ten, get lost,' whatever. They loved it. I was all spunky. A couple of them were pretty cute even, and the attention was great. I felt safe—lots of people hanging around, they weren't going to try anything funny. Only I was starting to freak out about the car—it was really dead. I'd reseated everything, self-tested every component, double-checked the fuel. Nothing nothing nothing! I was going to have to call a tow and my mom was going to kill me.

"So I'm trying not to let it get to me, trying to keep it all cool, but I'm not doing a great job. The frat guys are all standing too close and they smell like beer, and I'm not trying to be perky anymore, just want them to stay! away! but they won't back off. I'm trying not to cry.

"And then the cops showed up. Not real cops, but Sony's Vehicle Recovery Squad. All dressed up in Vaio gear, stylish as a Pepsi ad, packing lots of semilethals and silvery aeorosol shut-up-and-be-still juice, ready to nab the bad, bad perp who boosted this lovely Veddic Series 7 from Mom's lot. Part of the franchise package, that kind of response. It took me a second to figure it out—Mom didn't know it was *me* who had the car, so she'd called in a theft and bam, I was about to get arrested. The frat rats tried to run away, which is a bad idea, you just don't ever run from cops—stupid, stupid, stupid. They ended up rolling around on the ground, screaming and trying to pull their faces off. It took, like a second. I threw my hands in the air. 'Don't shoot!' They gassed me anyway.

"So then *I* was rolling around on the ground, feeling like my sinuses were trying to explode out of my face. Feeling like my eyeballs were melting. Feeling like my lungs were all shriveled up into raisins. I couldn't scream, I couldn't even breathe. By the time I could even roll over and open my eyes, they had me cuffed: ankles and wrists in zapstraps that were so tight, they felt like piano wire. I was a cool fifteen-year-old, but not that cool. I started up the water-works, boohoohoo, couldn't shut it down, couldn't even get angry. I just wanted to die. The Sony cops had seen it all before, so they put a tarp down on the Veddic's backseat upholstery, threw me in it, then rolled it into their recovery truck and drove me to the police station.

"I puked on the tarp twice before they got me there, and almost did it a third time on the way to booking. It got up my sinuses and down my throat, too. I couldn't stop gagging, couldn't stop crying, but by now I was getting pissed. I'd been raised on the whole Sony message: 'A Car for the Rest of Us,' gone with Mom to their Empowerment Seminars, wore the little tee shirts and the temporary tats and chatted up the tire-kickers about the Sony Family while Mom was busy. This wasn't the Sony Family I knew.

"I was tied up on the floor beside the desk sergeant's counter, and a Sony cop was filling in my paperwork, and so I spat out the crud from my mouth, stopped sniveling, hawked back my spit and put on my best voice. 'This isn't necessary, sir,' I said. 'I'm not a thief. My mother owns the dealership. It was wrong to take the car, but I'm sure she didn't intend for this to happen. Certainly, I don't need to be tied up in here. Please, take off the restraints—they're cutting off my circulation.' The Sony cop flipped up his goofy little facemask and squinted at me, then shook his head and went back to his paperwork.

"'Look,' I said. 'Look! I'm not a criminal. This is a misunderstanding. If you check my ID and call my mother, we can work this all out. Look!' I read his name off his chest. 'Look! Officer Langtree! Just let me up and we'll sort this out like adults. Come on, I don't blame you—I'm glad!—you were right to take me in. This is my mom's merchandise; it's good that you went after the thief and recovered the car. But now you know the truth, it's my mother's car, and if you just let me up, I'm sure we can work this out. Please, Officer Langtree. My wallet's in my back pocket. Just get it out and check my ID before you do this.'

"But he just went on filling in the paperwork. 'Why? Why won't you just take a second to check? Why not?'

"He turned around again, looked at me for a long time, and I was sure he was going to check, that it was all going to be fine, but then he said, 'Look, I've had about as much of your bullshit as I'm going to take, little girl. Shut your hole or I'll gag you. I just want to get out of here and back to my job, all right?'

"'What?' I said, and it sounded like a shriek to me. 'What did you say to me? What the hell did you say to me? Didn't you hear what I said? That's my *mother's car*—she owns the lot I took it off of. Do you honestly think she wants you to do this? This is the stupidest goddamned thing—'

"'That's it,' he said, and took a little silver micropore hood off his belt, the kind that you cinch up under the chin so the person inside can't talk? I started squirming away then, pleading with him, and I finally caught the desk sergeant's eye. 'He can't do this! Please! Don't let him do this! I'm in a *police station*—why are you letting him do this?'

"And the cop smiled and said, 'You're absolutely right, little girl. That's enough of that.' The Sony cop didn't pay any attention. He grabbed my head and stuffed it into the hood and tried to get the chin strap in place. I shook my head as best as I could, and then the hood was being taken off my head again, and the

Sony cop looked like he wanted to nail the other cop, but he didn't. The desk sergeant bent down and cut my straps, then helped me to my feet.

"'You're not going to give me any trouble, are you?' he said, as he led me around to a nice, ergo office chair.

"'No sir!'

"'You just sit there, then, and I'll be with you in a moment.'

"I sat down and rubbed my wrists and ankles. My left ankle was oozing blood from where it had been rubbed raw. I couldn't believe that the Sony Family could inflict such indignities on my cute little person. I was so goddamn self-righteous, and I know I was smirking as the desk sergeant chewed out the Sony cop, taking down his badge number and so on so that I'd have it.

"I thanked the cop profusely, and I kept on thanking him as he booked me and printed me and took my mug shots. I was joking and maybe even flirting a little. I was a cute fifteen-year-old and I knew it. After the nastiness with the Sony cops, being processed into the criminal justice system seemed mild and inoffensive. It didn't really occur to me that I was being *arrested* until my good pal the cop asked me to turn out my pockets before he put me in the cell.

"'Wait!' I said. 'Sergeant Lorenzi, wait! You don't have to put me in a *cell*, do you, Sergeant Lorenzi? Sergeant Lorenzi! I don't need to go into a cell! Let me call my mom, she'll come down and drop the charges, and I can wait here. I'll help out. I can get coffee. Sergeant Lorenzi!'

"For a second, it looked like he was going to go through with it. Then he relented and I spent the next couple hours fetching and filing and even running out for coffee—that's how much he trusted me—while we waited for Mom to show up. I was actually feeling pretty good about it by the time she arrived. Of course, that didn't last too long.

"She came through the door like Yosemite Sam, frothing at the chops and howling for my blood. She wanted to press charges, see me locked up to teach me a lesson. She didn't care how the Sony cops had gassed and trussed me—as far as she was concerned, I'd betrayed her and nothing was going to make it right. She kept howling for the sergeant to give her the papers to sign, she wanted to swear out a complaint, and he just let her run out of steam, his face perfectly expressionless until she was done.

"'All right then, Mrs. Walchuk, all right. You swear out the complaint, and we'll hold her overnight until her bail hearing. We only got the one holding cell, though, you understand. No juvenile facility. Rough crowd. A couple of biowar enthusiasts in there right now, caught 'em trying to thrax a bus terminal; a girl who killed her pimp and nailed his privates to the door of his hotel room before she took off; a couple of hard old drunks. No telling what else will come in today. We take away their knives and boots and purses, but those girls like to mess up fresh young things, scar them with the bars or their nails. We can't watch them all the time.' He was leaning right across the desk at my mom, cold and still, and then he nudged my foot with his foot and I knew that he was yanking her chain.

"'Is that what you want, then, ma'am?'

"Mom looked like she wanted to tell him yes, go ahead, call his bluff, but he was too good at it. She broke. 'No, it's not,' she said. 'I'll take her home and deal with her there.'

"'That's fundamentally sound,' he said. 'And Linda, you give me a call if you want to file a complaint against Sony. We have secam footage of the Boardwalk and the Station House if you need it, and I have that guy's badge ID, too.'

"Mom looked alarmed, and I held out my raw, bruisey wrists to her. 'They gassed me before they took me in.'

"'Did you run? You *never* run from the cops, Linda, you should have known better—'

"I didn't run. I put my arms in the air and they gassed me and tied me up and took me in.'

"'That can't be, Linda. You must have done *something*—' Mom always was ready to believe that I deserved whatever trouble I got into. She was the only one who didn't care how cute I was.

"'No mom. I put my hands in the air. I surrendered. They got me anyway. They didn't care. It'll be on the tape. I'll get it from Sergeant Lorenzi when I file my complaint.'

"'You'll do no such thing. You stole a car, you endangered lives, and now you want to go sniveling to the authorities because Sony played a little rough when they brought you in? You committed a *criminal act*, Linda. You got treated like a criminal.'

"I wanted to smack her. I knew that this was really about not embarrassing her in front of the Sony Family, the nosy chattery ladies with the other franchises that Mom competed against for brownie points and bragging rights. But I'd learned something about drawing flies with honey that afternoon. The sergeant could have made things very hard on me, but by giving him a little sugar, I turned it into an almost fun afternoon.

"Mom took me home and screamed herself raw, and I played it all very contrite, then walked over to the minimall so that I could buy some saline solution for my eyes, which were still as red as stoplights. We never spoke of it again, and on my sixteenth birthday, Mom gave me the keys to a Veddic Series 8, and the first thing I did was download new firmware for the antitheft transponder that killed it. Two months later, it was stolen. I haven't driven a Sony since."

Linda smiles and then purses her lips. "Unrehearsed enough?"

Art shakes his head. "Wow. What a story."

"Do you want to kiss me now?" Linda says, conversationally.

"I believe I do," Art says, and he does.

Linda pulls the back of his head to hers with one

arm, and with the other, she half-shrugs out her robe. Art pulls his shirt up to his armpits, feels the scorching softness of her chest on his, and groans. His erection grinds into her mons through his Jockey shorts, and he groans again as she sucks his tongue into her mouth and masticates it just shy of hard enough to hurt.

She breaks off and reaches down for the waistband of his Jockeys and his whole body arches in anticipation.

Then his comm rings.

Again.

"Fuck!" Art says, just as Linda says, "Shit!" and they both snort a laugh. Linda pulls his hand to her nipple again and Art shivers, sighs, and reaches for his comm, which won't stop ringing.

"It's me," Fede says.

"Jesus, Fede. What *is it?*"

"What is it? Art, you haven't been to the office for more than four hours in a week. It's going on noon, and you still aren't here." Fede's voice is hot and unreasoning.

Art feels his own temper rise in response. Where the hell did Fede get off, anyway? "So fucking *what,* Fede? I don't actually work for you, you know. I've been taking care of stuff offsite."

"Oh, sure. Art, if you get in trouble, I'll get in trouble, and you know *exactly* what I mean."

"I'm not *in* trouble, Fede. I'm taking the day off— why don't you call me tomorrow?"

"What the hell does that mean? You can't just 'take the day off.' I *wrote* the goddamned procedure. You have to fill in the form and get it signed by your supervisor. It needs to be *documented*. Are you *trying* to undermine me?"

"You are so goddamned *paranoid*, Federico. I got mugged last night, all right? I've been in a police station for the past eighteen hours straight. I am going to take a shower and I am going to take a nap and I am going to get a massage, and I am *not* going into the office and I am *not* going to fill in any forms. This is not about you."

Fede pauses for a moment, and Art senses him marshalling his bad temper for another salvo. "I don't give a shit, Art. If you're not coming into the office, you tell me, you hear? The VP of HR is going berserk, and I know exactly what it's about. He is on to us, you hear me? Every day that you're away and I'm covering for your ass, he gets more and more certain. If you keep this shit up, we're both dead."

"Hey, fuck you, Fede." Art is surprised to hear the words coming out of his mouth, but once they're out, he decides to go with them. "You can indulge your paranoid fantasies to your heart's content, but don't drag me into them. I got mugged last night. I had a near-fatal car crash a couple weeks ago. If the VP of HR wants to find out why I haven't been in the office, he can send me an email and I'll tell him exactly what's going on, and if he doesn't like it, he can toss my goddamned salad. But I don't report to you. If you want to have a discussion, you call me and act like a human goddamned being. Tomorrow. Goodbye, Fede." Art rings the comm off and snarls at it, then switches it off, switches off the emergency override, and briefly considers tossing it out the goddamned window onto the precious English paving stones below. Instead, he hurls it into the soft cushions of the sofa.

He turns back to Linda and makes a conscious effort to wipe the snarl off his face. He ratchets a smile onto his lips. "Sorry, sorry. Last time, I swear." He crawls over to her on all fours. She's pulled her robe tight around her, and he slides a finger under the collar and slides it aside and darts in for a kiss on the hollow of her collarbone. She shies away and drops her cheek to her shoulder, shielding his target.

"I'm not—" she starts. "The moment's passed, OK? Why don't we just cuddle, OK?"

> > > > > > > > > > > **12**

Art was at his desk at O'Malley House the next day when Fede knocked on his door. Fede was bearing a small translucent gift-bag made of some cunning combination of rough handmade paper and slick polymer. Art looked up from his comm and waved at the door.

Fede came in and put the parcel on Art's desk. Art looked askance at Fede, and Fede just waved at the bag with a go-ahead gesture. Art felt for the catch that would open the bag without tearing the materials, couldn't find it immediately, and reflexively fired up his comm and started to make notes on how a revised version of the bag could provide visual cues showing how to open it. Fede caught him at it and they traded grins.

Art probed the bag's orifice a while longer, then happened upon the release. The bag sighed apart, falling in three petals, and revealed its payload: a small, leather-worked box with a simple brass catch. Art flipped the catch and eased the box open. Inside, in a fitted foam cavity, was a gray lump of stone.

"It's an axe head," Fede said. "It's 200,000 years old."

Art lifted it out of the box carefully and turned it about, admiring the clean tool marks from its shaping. It had heft and brutal simplicity, and a thin spot where a handle must have been lashed once upon a time. Art ran his fingertips over the smooth tool marks, over the tapered business end, where the stone had been painstakingly flaked into an edge. It was perfect.

Now that he was holding it, it was so obviously an axe, so clearly an axe. It needed no instruction. It explained itself. I am an axe. Hit things with me. Art couldn't think of a single means by which it could be improved.

"Fede," he said, "Fede, this is incredible—"

"I figured we needed to bury the hatchet, huh?"

"God, that's awful. Here's a tip: When you give a gift like this, just leave humor out of it, OK? You don't have the knack." Art slapped him on the shoulder to show him he was kidding, and reverently returned the axe to its cavity. "That is really one hell of a gift, Fede. Thank you."

Fede stuck his hand out. Art shook it, and some of the week's tension melted away.

"Now, you're going to buy me lunch," Fede said.

"Deal."

They toddled off to Piccadilly and grabbed seats at the counter of a South Indian place for a businessmen's lunch of thali and thick mango lassi, which coated their tongues in alkaline sweetness that put out the flames from the spiced veggies. Both men were sweating by the time they ordered their second round of lassi and Art had his hands on his belly, amazed as ever that something as insubstantial as the little platter's complement of veggies and naan could fill him as efficiently as it had.

"What are you working on now?" Fede asked, suppressing a curry-whiffing belch.

"Same shit," Art said. "There are a million ways to make the service work. The rights-societies want lots of accounting and lots of pay-per-use. MassPike hates that. It's a pain in the ass to manage, and the clickthrough licenses and warnings they want to slap on are heinous. People are going to crash their cars fucking around with the 'I Agree' buttons. Not to mention they want to require a firmware check on every stereo system that gets a song, make sure that this week's copy-protection is installed. So I'm coopering up all these user studies with weasels from the legal departments at the studios, where they just slaver all over this stuff, talking about how warm it all makes them feel to make sure that they're compensating artists and how grateful they are for the reminders to keep their software up to date and shit. I'm modeling a system that has a clickthrough every time you cue up a new song, too. It's going to be perfect: the rights-societies are going to love it, and I've handpicked the peer review group at V/DT, stacked it up with total assholes who love manuals and following rules. It's going to sail through approval."

Fede grunted. "You don't think it'll be too obvious?"

Art laughed. "There is no such thing as too obvious in this context, man. These guys, they hate the end-user, and for years they've been getting away with it because all their users are already used to being treated like shit at the post office and the tube station. I mean, these people grew up with *coin-operated stoves*, for chrissakes! They pay television tax! Feed 'em shit and they'll ask you for second helpings. Beg you for 'em! So no, I don't think it'll be too obvious. They'll mock up the whole system and march right into MassPike with it, grinning like idiots. Don't worry about a thing."

"OK, OK. I get it. I won't worry."

Art signalled the counterman for their bill. The counterman waved distractedly in the manner of a harried restaurateur dealing with his regulars, and said something in Korean to the busgirl, who along with the Vietnamese chef and the Congolese sous chef, lent the joint a transworld sensibility that made it a favorite among the painfully global darlings of O'Malley House. The busgirl found a pad and started totting up numbers, then keyed them into a point-of-sale terminal, which juiced Art's comm with an accounting for their lunch. This business with hand-noting everything before entering it into the PoS had driven Art to distraction when he'd first encountered it. He'd assumed that the terminal's UI was such that a computer-illiterate busgirl couldn't reliably key in the data without having it in front of her, and for months he'd cited it in net-bullshit sessions as more evidence of the pervasive user-hostility that charac-terized the whole damned GMT.

He'd finally tried out his rant on the counterman, one foreigner to another, just a little Briton-bashing session between two refugees from the Colonial Jack-boot. To his everlasting surprise, the counterman had vigorously defended the system, saying that he liked the PoS data-entry system just fine, and that the stack of torn-off paper stubs from the busgirl's receipt book was a good visualization tool, letting him eyeball the customer volume from hour to hour by checking the spike beside the till, and the rubberbanded stacks of yellowing paper lining his cellar's shelves gave him a wonderfully physical evidence of the growing success of his little eatery. There was a lesson there, Art knew, though he'd yet to codify it. User mythology was tricky that way.

Every time Art scribbled a tip into his comm and squirted it back at the PoS, he considered this little puzzle, eyes unfocusing for a moment while his vision turned inwards. As his eyes snapped back into focus, he noticed the young lad sitting on the long leg of the ell formed by the counter. He had bully short hair and broad shoulders, and a sneer that didn't quite disappear as he shoveled up the dhal with his biodegradable bamboo disposable spork.

He knew that guy from somewhere. The guy caught him staring and they locked eyes for a moment, and in that instant Art knew who the guy was. It was Tom, whom he had last seen stabbing at him with a tazer clutched in one shaking fist, face twisted in fury. Tom wasn't wearing his killsport armor, just nondescript athletic wear, and he wasn't with Lester and Tony, but it was him. Art watched Tom cock his head to jog his memory, and then saw Tom recognize him. Uh-oh.

"We have to go. Now," he said to Fede, standing and walking away quickly, hand going to his comm. He stopped short of dialing 999, though—he wasn't up for another police-station all-nighter. He got halfway up Piccadilly before looking over his shoulder, and he saw Fede shouldering his way through the lunchtime crowd, looking pissed. A few paces behind him came Tom, face contorted in a sadistic snarl.

Art did a little two-step of indecision, moving towards Fede, then away from him. He met Tom's eyes again, and Tom's ferocious, bared teeth spurred him on. He turned abruptly into the tube station, waved his comm at a turnstile and dove into the thick of the crowd heading down the escalator to the Bakerloo Line. His comm rang.

"What is *wrong* with you, man?" Fede said.

"One of the guys who mugged me," he hissed. "He was sitting right across from us. He's a couple steps behind you. I'm in the tube station. I'll ride a stop and catch a cab back to the office."

"He's behind me? Where?"

Art's comm lit up with a grainy feed from Fede's comm. It jiggled as Fede hustled through the crowd.

"Jesus, Fede, stop! Don't go to the goddamned tube station—he'll follow you here."

"Where do you want me to go? I got to go back to the office."

"Don't go there either. Get a cab and circle the block a couple times. Don't lead him back."

"This is stupid. Why don't I just call the cops?"

"Don't bother. They won't do shit. I've been through this already. I just want to lose that guy and not have him find me again later."

"Christ."

Art squeaked as Tom filled his screen, then passed by, swinging his head from side to side with saurian rage.

"What?" Fede said.

"That was him. He just walked past you. He must not know you're with me. Go back to the office, I'll meet you there."

"That dipshit? Art, he's all of five feet tall!"

"He's a fucking psycho, Fede. Don't screw around with him or he'll give you a Tesla enema."

Fede winced. "I hate tazers."

"The train is pulling in. I'll talk to you later."

"OK, OK."

Art formed up in queue with the rest of the passengers and shuffled through the gas chromatograph, tensing up a little as it sniffed his personal space for black powder residue. Once on board, he tore a sani-wipe from the roll in the ceiling, ignoring the V/DT ad on it, and grabbed the stainless steel rail with it, stamping on the drifts of sani-wipe mulch on the train's floor.

He made a conscious effort to control his breathing, willed his heart to stop pounding. He was still juiced with adrenaline, and his mind raced. He needed to do something constructive with his time, but his mind kept wandering. Finally, he gave in and let it wander.

Something about the counterman, about his slips

of paper, about the MassPike. It was knocking around in his brain and he just couldn't figure out how to bring it to the fore. The counterman kept his slips in the basement so that he could sit among them and see how his business had grown, every slip a person served, a ring on the till, money in the bank. Drivers on the MassPike who used traffic jams to download music from nearby cars and then paid to license the songs. Only they didn't. They circumvented the payment system in droves, running bootleg operations out of their cars that put poor old Napster to shame for sheer volume. Some people drove in promiscuous mode, collecting every song in every car on the turnpike, cruising the tunnels that riddled Boston like mobile pirate radio stations, dumping their collections to other drivers when it came time to quit the turnpike and settle up for their music at the toll booth.

It was these war-drivers that MassPike was really worried about. Admittedly, they actually made the system go. Your average fartmobile driver had all of ten songs in his queue, and the short-range, broadband connection you had on MassPike meant that if you were stuck in a jam of these cars, your selection would be severely limited. The war-drivers, though, were mobile jukeboxes. The highway patrol had actually seized cars with over 300,000 tracks on their drives. Without these fat caches on the highway, MassPike would have to spend a fortune on essentially replicating the system with their own mobile libraries.

The war-drivers were the collective memory of the MassPike's music-listeners.

Ooh, there was a tasty idea. The collective memory of MassPike. Like Dark Ages scholars, memorizing entire texts to preserve them against the depredations of barbarism, passing their collections carefully from car to car. He'd investigated the highway patrol reports on these guys, and there were hints there, shadowy clues of an organized subculture, one with a hierarchy, where newbies tricked out their storage with libraries of novel and rare tuneage in a bid to convince the established elite that they were worthy of joining the collective memory.

Thinking of war-drivers as a collective memory was like staring at an optical illusion and seeing the vase emerge from the two faces. Art's entire perception of the problem involuted itself in his mind. He heard panting and realized it was him; he was hyperventilating.

If these guys were the collective memory of the MassPike, that meant that they were performing a service, reducing MassPike's costs significantly. That meant that they were tastemakers, injecting fresh music into the static world of Boston drivers. Mmmm. Trace that. Find out how influential they were. Someone would know—the MassPike had stats on how songs migrated from car to car. Even without investigating it, Art just *knew* that these guys were offsetting millions of dollars in marketing.

So. So. So. So, *feed* that culture. War-drivers needed to be devoted to make it into the subculture. They had to spend four or five hours a day cruising the freeways to accumulate and propagate their collections. They couldn't *leave* the MassPike until they found someone to hand their collections off to.

What if MassPike *rewarded* these guys? What if MassPike charged *nothing* for anyone with more than, say 50,000 tunes in their cache? Art whipped out his comm and his keyboard and started making notes, snatching at the silver rail with his keyboard hand every time the train jerked and threatened to topple him. That's how the tube cops found him, once the train reached Elephant and Castle and they did their rounds, politely but firmly rousting him.

>>>>>>>>>>13

I am already in as much trouble as I can be, I think. I have left my room, hit and detonated some poor cafeteria hash-slinger's fartmobile, and certainly damned some hapless secret smoker to employee Hades for his security lapses. When I get down from here, I will be bound up in a chemical straitjacket. I'll be one of the ward-corner droolers, propped up in a wheelchair in front of the video, tended twice daily for diaper changes, feeding and re-medication.

That is the worst they can do, and I'm in for it. This leaves me asking two questions:

1. Why am I so damned eager to be rescued from my rooftop aerie? I am sunburned and sad, but I am more free than I have been in weeks.
2. Why am I so reluctant to take further action in the service of getting someone up onto the roof? I could topple a ventilator chimney by moving the cinderblocks that hold its apron down and giving it the shoulder. I could dump rattling handfuls of gravel down its maw and wake the psychotics below.

I could, but I won't. Maybe I don't want to go back just yet.

They cooked it up between them. The Jersey customers, Fede, and Linda. I should have known better.

When I landed at Logan, I was full of beans, ready to design and implement my war-driving scheme for the Jersey customers and advance the glorious cause of the Eastern Standard Tribe. I gleefully hopped up and down the coast, chilling in Manhattan for a day or two, hanging out with Gran in Toronto.

That Linda followed me out made it all even better. We rented cars and drove them from city to city, dropping them off at the city limits and switching to top-grade EST public transit, eating top-grade EST pizza, heads turning to follow the impeccably dressed, buff couples that strolled the pedestrian-friendly streets arm in arm. We sat on stoops in Brooklyn with old ladies who talked softly in the gloaming of the pollution-tinged sunsets while their grandchildren chased each other down the street. We joined a pickup game of street-hockey in Boston, yelling "Car!" and clearing the net every time a fartmobile turned into the cul-de-sac.

We played like kids. I got commed during working hours and my evenings were blissfully devoid of buzzes, beeps and alerts. It surprised the hell out of me when I discovered Fede's treachery and Linda's complicity and found myself flying cattle class to London to kick Fede's ass. What an idiot I am.

I have never won an argument with Fede. I thought I had that time, of course, but I should have known better. I was hardly back in Boston for a day before the men with the white coats came to take me away.

They showed up at the Novotel, soothing and grim, and opened my room's keycard reader with a mental-hygiene override. There were four of them, wiry and fast with the no-nonsense manner of men who have been unexpectedly hammered by outwardly calm psychopaths. That I was harmlessly having a rare cigarette on the balcony, dripping from the shower, made no impression on them. They dropped their faceplates, moved quickly to the balcony and boxed me in.

One of them recited a Miranda-esque litany that ended with "Do you understand." It wasn't really a question, but I answered anyway. "No! No I don't!

Who the hell are you, and what are you doing in my fucking hotel room?"

In my heart, though, I knew. I'd lived enough of my life on the hallucinatory edge of sleepdep to have anticipated this moment during a thousand freak-outs. I was being led away to the sanatorium, because someone, somewhere, had figured out about the scurrying hamsters in my brain. About time.

As soon as I said the *eff*-word, the guns came out. I tried to relax. I knew intuitively that this could either be a routine and impersonal affair, or a screaming, kicking, biting nightmare. I knew that arriving at the intake in a calm frame of mind would make the difference between a chemical straitjacket and a sleeping pill.

The guns were nonlethals, and varied: two kinds of nasty aerosol, a dart-gun, and a tazer. The tazer captured my attention, whipping horizontal lightning in the spring breeze. The Tesla enema, they called it in London. Supposedly club-kids used them recreationally, but everyone I knew who'd been hit with one described the experience as fundamentally and uniquely horrible.

I slowly raised my hands. "I would like to pack a bag, and I would like to see documentary evidence of your authority. May I?" I kept my voice as calm as I could, but it cracked on "May I?"

The reader of the litany nodded slowly. "You tell us what you want packed and we'll pack it. Once that's done, I'll show you the committal document, all right?"

"Thank you," I said.

They drove me through the Route 128 traffic in the sealed and padded compartment in the back of their van. I was strapped in at the waist, and strapped over with my shoulders with a padded harness that reminded me of a rollercoaster restraint. We made slow progress, jerking and changing lanes at regular intervals. The traffic signature of 128 was unmistakable.

The intake doctor wanded me for contraband, drew fluids from my various parts, and made light chitchat with me along the way. It was the last time I saw him. Before I knew it, a beefy orderly had me by the arm and was leading me to my room. He had a thick Eastern European accent, and he ran down the house rules for me in battered English. I tried to devote my attention to it, to forget the slack-eyed ward denizens I'd passed on my way in. I succeeded enough to understand the relationship of my legcuff, the door frame and the elevators. The orderly fished in his smock and produced a hypo.

"For sleepink," he said.

Panic, suppressed since my arrival, welled up and burst over. "Wait!" I said. "What about my things? I had a bag with me."

"Talk to doctor in morning," he said, gesturing with the hypo, fitting it with a needle-and-dosage cartridge and popping the sterile wrap off with a thumb-switch. "Now, for sleepink." He advanced on me.

I'd been telling myself that this was a chance to

rest, to relax and gather my wits. Soon enough, I'd sort things out with the doctors and I'd be on my way. I'd argue my way out of it. But here came Boris Badinoff with his magic needle, and all reason fled. I scrambled back over the bed and pressed against the window.

"It's barely three," I said, guessing at the time in the absence of my comm. "I'm not tired. I'll go to sleep when I am."

"For sleepink," he repeated, in a more soothing tone.

"No, that's all right. I'm tired enough. Long night last night. I'll just lie down and nap now, all right? No need for needles, OK?"

He grabbed my wrist. I tried to tug it out of his grasp, to squirm away. There's a lot of good, old-fashioned dirty fighting in Tai Chi—eye-gouging, groin punches, hold-breaks and come-alongs—and they all fled me. I thrashed like a fish on a line as he ran the hypo over the crook of my elbow until the vein-sensing LED glowed white. He jabbed down with it and I felt a prick. For a second, I thought that it hadn't taken effect—I've done enough chemical sleep in my years with the Tribe that I've developed quite a tolerance for most varieties—but then I felt that unmistakable heaviness in my eyelids, the melatonin crash that signalled the onslaught of merciless rest. I collapsed into bed.

I spent the next day in a drugged stupor. I've become quite accustomed to functioning in a stupor over the years, but this was different. No caffeine, for starters. They fed me and I had a meeting with a nice doctor who ran it down for me. I was here for observation pending a competency hearing in a week. I had seven days to prove that I wasn't a danger to myself or others, and if I could, the judge would let me go.

"It's like I'm a drug addict, huh?" I said to the doctor, who was used to non sequiturs.

"Sure, sure it is." He shifted in the hard chair opposite my bed, getting ready to go.

"No, really, I'm not just running my mouth. It's like this: *I* don't think I have a problem here. I think that my way of conducting my life is perfectly harmless. Like a speedfreak who thinks that she's just having a great time, being ultraproductive and coming out ahead of the game. But her friends, they're convinced she's destroying herself—they see the danger she's putting herself in, they see her health deteriorating. So they put her into rehab, kicking and screaming, where she stays until she figures it out.

"So, it's like I'm addicted to being nuts. I have a nonrational view of the world around me. An *inaccurate* view. You are meant to be the objective observer, to make such notes as are necessary to determine if I'm seeing things properly, or through a haze of nutziness. For as long as I go on taking my drug— shooting up my craziness—you keep me here. Once I stop, once I accept the objective truth of reality, you let me go. What then? Do I become a recovering nutcase? Do I have to stand ever-vigilant against the siren song of craziness?"

The doctor ran his hands through his long hair and bounced his knee up and down. "You could put it that way, I guess."

"So tell me, what's the next step? What is my optimum strategy for providing compelling evidence of my repudiation of my worldview?"

"Well, that's where the analogy breaks down. This isn't about anything demonstrable. There's no one thing we look for in making our diagnosis. It's a collection of things, a protocol for evaluating you. It doesn't happen overnight, either. You were committed on the basis of evidence that you had made threats to your coworkers due to a belief that they were seeking to harm you."

"Interesting. Can we try a little thought experiment, Doctor? Say that your coworkers really *were* seeking to harm you—this is not without historical precedent, right? They're seeking to sabotage you because you've discovered some terrible treachery on their part, and they want to hush you up. So they provoke a reaction from you and use it as the basis for an involuntary committal. How would you, as a medical professional, distinguish that scenario from one in which the patient is genuinely paranoid and delusional?"

The doctor looked away. "It's in the protocol—we find it there."

"I see," I said, moving in for the kill. "I see. Where would I get more information on the protocol? I'd like to research it before my hearing."

"I'm sorry," the doctor said, "we don't provide access to medical texts to our patients."

"Why not? How can I defend myself against a charge if I'm not made aware of the means by which my defense is judged? That hardly seems fair."

The doctor stood and smoothed his coat, turned his badge's lanyard so that his picture faced outwards. "Art, you're not here to defend yourself. You're here so that we can take a look at you and understand what's going on. If you have been set up, we'll discover it—"

"What's the ratio of real paranoids to people who've been set up, in your experience?"

"I don't keep stats on that sort of thing—"

"How many paranoids have been released because they were vindicated?"

"I'd have to go through my case histories—"

"Is it more than ten?"

"No, I wouldn't think so—"

"More than five?"

"Art, I don't think—"

"Have *any* paranoids ever been vindicated? Is this observation period anything more than a formality en route to committal? Come on, Doctor, just let me know where I stand."

"Art, we're on your side here. If you want to make this easy on yourself, then you should understand that. The nurse will be in with your lunch and your meds in a few minutes, then you'll be allowed out on the ward. I'll speak to you there more, if you want."

"Doctor, it's a simple question: Has anyone ever been admitted to this facility because it was believed he had paranoid delusions, and later released because he was indeed the center of a plot?"

"Art, it's not appropriate for me to discuss other patients' histories—"

"Don't you publish case studies? Don't those contain confidential information disguised with pseudonyms?"

"That's not the point—"

"What *is* the point? It seems to me that my optimal strategy here is to repudiate my belief that Fede and Linda are plotting against me—*even* if I still believe this to be true, even if it *is* true—and profess a belief that they are my good and concerned friends. In other words, if they are indeed plotting against me, I must profess to a delusional belief that they aren't, in order to prove that I am not delusional."

"I read *Catch-22* too, Art. That's not what this is about, but your attitude isn't going to help you any here." The doctor scribbled on his comm briefly, tapped at some menus. I leaned across and stared at the screen.

"That looks like a prescription, Doctor."

"It is. I'm giving you a mild sedative. We can't help you until you're calmer and ready to listen."

"I'm perfectly calm. I just disagree with you. I am the sort of person who learns through debate. Medication won't stop that."

"We'll see," the doctor said, and left, before I could muster a riposte.

I was finally allowed onto the ward, dressed in what the nurses called "day clothes"—the civilian duds that I'd packed before leaving the hotel, which an orderly retrieved for me from a locked closet in my room. The clustered nuts were watching slackjaw TV, or staring out the windows, or rocking in place, fidgeting and muttering. I found myself a seat next to a birdy woman whose long, oily hair was parted down the middle, leaving a furrow in her scalp lined with twin rows of dandruff. She was young, maybe twenty-five, and seemed the least stuporous of the lot.

"Hello," I said to her.

She smiled shyly, then pitched forward and vomited copiously and noisily between her knees. I shrank back and struggled to keep my face neutral. A nurse hastened to her side and dropped a plastic bucket in the stream of puke, which was still gushing out of her mouth, her thin chest heaving.

"Here, Sarah, in here," the nurse said, with an air of irritation.

"Can I help?" I said, ridiculously.

She looked sharply at me. "Art, isn't it? Why aren't you in Group? It's after one!"

"Group?" I asked.

"Group. In that corner, there." She gestured at a collection of sagging sofas underneath one of the ward's grilled-in windows. "You're late, and they've started without you."

There were four other people there, two women and a young boy, and a doctor in mufti, identifiable by his shoes—not slippers—and his staff of office, the almighty badge-on-a-lanyard.

Throbbing with dread, I moved away from the still-heaving girl to the sofa cluster and stood at its edge. The group turned to look at me. The doctor cleared his throat. "Group, this is Art. Glad you made it, Art. You're a little late, but we're just getting started here, so that's OK. This is Lucy, Fatima, and Manuel. Why don't you have a seat?" His voice was professionally smooth and stultifying.

I sank into a bright orange sofa that exhaled a cloud of dust motes that danced in the sun streaming through the windows. It also exhaled a breath of trapped ancient farts, barf-smell, and antiseptic, the *parfum de asylum* that gradually numbed my nose to all other scents on the ward. I folded my hands in my lap and tried to look attentive.

"All right, Art. Everyone in the group is pretty new here, so you don't have to worry about not knowing what's what. There are no right or wrong things. The only rules are that you can't interrupt anyone, and if you want to criticize, you have to criticize the idea, and not the person who said it. All right?"

"Sure," I said. "Sure. Let's get started."

"Well, aren't you eager?" the doctor said warmly. "OK. Manuel was just telling us about his friends."

"They're not my friends," Manuel said angrily. "They're the reason I'm here. I hate them."

"Go on," the doctor said.

"I already *told* you, yesterday! Tony and Musafir, they're trying to get rid of me. I make them look bad, so they want to get rid of me."

"Why do you think you make them look bad?"

"Because I'm better than them—I'm smarter, I dress better, I get better grades, I score more goals. The girls like me better. They hate me for it."

"Oh yeah, you're the cat's ass, pookie," Lucy said. She was about fifteen, voluminously fat, and her full lips twisted in an elaborate sneer as she spoke.

"Lucy," the doctor said patiently, favoring her with a patronizing smile. "That's not cool, OK? Criticize the idea, not the person, and only when it's your turn, OK?"

Lucy rolled her eyes with the eloquence of teen-agedom.

"All right, Manuel, thank you. Group, do you have any positive suggestions for Manuel?"

Stony silence.

"OK! Manuel, some of us are good at some things, and some of us are good at others. Your friends don't hate you, and I'm sure that if you think about it, you'll know that you don't hate them. Didn't they come visit you last weekend? Successful people are well liked, and you're no exception. We'll come back to this tomorrow—why don't you spend the time until then thinking of three examples of how your friends showed you that they liked you, and you can tell us about it tomorrow?"

Manuel stared out the window.

"OK! Now, Art, welcome again. Tell us why you're here."

"I'm in for observation. There's a competency hearing at the end of the week."

Lisa snorted and Fatima giggled.

The doctor ignored them. "But tell us *why* you think you ended up here."

"You want the whole story?"

"Whatever parts you think are important."

"It's a Tribal thing."

"I see," the doctor said.

"It's like this," I said. "It used to be that the way you chose your friends was by finding the most like-minded people you could out of the pool of people who lived near to you. If you were lucky, you lived near a bunch of people you could get along with. This was a lot more likely in the olden days, back before, you know, printing and radio and such. Chances were that you'd grow up so immersed in the local doctrine that you'd never even think to question it. If you were a genius or a psycho, you might come up with a whole new way of thinking, and if you could pull it off, you'd either gather up a bunch of people who liked your new idea or you'd go somewhere else, like America, where you could set up a little colony of people who agreed with you. Most of the time, though, people who didn't get along with their neighbors just moped around until they died."

"Very interesting," the doctor said, interrupting

smoothly, "but you were going to tell us how you ended up here."

"Yeah," Lucy said, "this isn't a history lesson, it's Group. Get to the point."

"I'm getting there," I said. "It just takes some background if you're going to understand it. Now, once ideas could travel more freely, the chances of you finding out about a group of people somewhere else that you might get along with increased. Like when my dad was growing up, if you were gay and from a big city, chances were that you could figure out where other gay people hung out and go and—" I waved my hands, "be *gay*, right? But if you were from a small town, you might not even know that there was such a thing as being gay—you might think it was just a perversion. But as time went by, the gay people in the big cities started making a bigger and bigger deal out of being gay, and since all the information that the small towns consumed came from big cities, that information leaked into the small towns and more gay people moved to the big cities, built little gay zones where gay was normal.

"So back when the New World was forming and sorting out its borders and territories, information was flowing pretty well. You had telegraphs, you had the Pony Express, you had thousands of little newspapers that got carried around on railroads and streetcars and steamers, and it wasn't long before everyone knew what kind of person went where, even back in Europe and Asia. People immigrated here and picked where they wanted to live based on what sort of people they wanted to be with, which ideas they liked best. A lot of it was religious, but that was just on the surface—underneath it all was aesthetics. You wanted to go somewhere where the girls were pretty in the way you understood prettiness, where the food smelled like food and not garbage, where shops sold goods you could recognize. Lots of other factors were at play, too, of course—jobs and Jim Crow laws and whatnot, but the tug of finding people like you is like gravity. Lots of things work against gravity, but gravity always wins in the end—in the end, everything collapses. In the end, everyone ends up with the people that are most like them that they can find."

I was warming to my subject now, in that flow state that great athletes get into when they just know where to swing their bat, where to plant their foot. I knew that I was working up a great rant.

"Fast-forward to the age of email. Slowly but surely, we begin to mediate almost all of our communication over networks. Why walk down the hallway to ask a coworker a question, when you can just send email? You don't need to interrupt them, and you can keep going on your own projects, and if you forget the answer, you can just open the message again and look at the response. There're all kinds of ways to interact with our friends over the network: we can play hallucinogenic games, chat, send pictures, code, music, funny articles, metric fuckloads of porn . . . The interaction is high-quality! Sure, you gain three pounds every year you spend behind the desk instead of walking down the hall to ask your buddy where he wants to go for lunch, but that's a small price to pay.

"So you're a fish out of water. You live in Arizona, but you're sixteen years old and all your neighbors are eighty-five, and you get ten billion channels of media on your desktop. All the good stuff—everything that tickles you—comes out of some clique of hyperurban club-kids in South Philly. They're making cool art, music, clothes. You read their mailing lists and you can tell that they're exactly the kind of people who'd really appreciate you for who you are. In the old days, you'd pack your bags and hitchhike across the country and move to your community. But you're sixteen, and that's a pretty scary step.

"Why move? These kids live online. At lunch, before school, and all night, they're comming in, talking trash, sending around photos, chatting. Online, you can be a peer. You can hop into these discussions, play the games, chord with one hand while chatting up some hottie a couple thousand miles away.

"Only you can't. You can't, because they chat at seven AM while they're getting ready for school. They chat at five PM, while they're working on their homework. Their late nights end at three AM. But those are their *local* times, not yours. If you get up at seven, they're already at school, 'cause it's ten there.

"So you start to *eff* with your sleep schedule. You get up at four AM so you can chat with your friends.

You go to bed at nine, 'cause that's when they go to bed. Used to be that it was stockbrokers and journos and factory workers who did that kind of thing, but now it's anyone who doesn't fit in. The geniuses and lunatics to whom the local doctrine tastes wrong. They choose their peers based on similarity, not geography, and they keep themselves awake at the same time as them. But you need to make some nod to localness, too—gotta be at work with everyone else, gotta get to the bank when it's open, gotta buy your groceries. You end up hardly sleeping at all, you end up sneaking naps in the middle of the day, or after dinner, trying to reconcile biological imperatives with cultural ones. Needless to say, that alienates you even further from the folks at home, and drives you more and more into the arms of your online peers of choice.

"So you get the Tribes. People all over the world who are really secret agents for some other time zone, some other way of looking at the world, some other zeitgeist. Unlike other tribes, you can change allegiance by doing nothing more than resetting your alarm clock. Like any tribe, they are primarily loyal to each other, and anyone outside of the tribe is only mostly human. That may sound extreme, but this is what it comes down to.

"Tribes are *agendas*. Aesthetics. Ethos. Traditions. Ways of getting things done. They're competitive. They may not all be based on time zones. There are knitting Tribes and vampire fan-fiction Tribes and Christian-rock Tribes, but they've always existed. Mostly, these tribes are little more than a subculture. It takes time zones to amplify the cultural fissioning of fan-fiction or knitting into a full-blown conspiracy. Their interests are commercial, industrial, cultural, culinary. A Tribesman will patronize a fellow Tribesman's restaurant, or give him a manufacturing contract, or hire his taxi. Not because of xenophobia, but because of homophilia: I know that my Tribesman's taxi will conduct its way through traffic in a way that I'm comfortable with, whether I'm in San Francisco, Boston, London or Calcutta. I know that the food will be palatable in a Tribal restaurant, that a book by a Tribalist will be a good read, that a gross of widgets will be manufactured to the exacting standards of my Tribe.

"Like I said, though, unless you're at ground zero, in the Tribe's native time zone, your sleep sched is just *raped*. You live on sleepdep and chat and secret agentry until it's second nature. You're cranky and subrational most of the time. Close your eyes on the freeway and dreams paint themselves on the back of your lids, demanding their time, almost as heavy as gravity, almost as remorseless. There's a lot of flaming and splitting and vitriol in the Tribes. They're more fractured than a potsherd. Tribal anthropologists have built up incredible histories of the fissioning of the Tribes since they were first recognized—most of 'em are online; you can look 'em up. We stab each other in the back routinely and with no more provocation than a sleepdep hallucination.

"Which is how I got here. I'm a member of the Eastern Standard Tribe. We're centered around New York, but we're ramified up and down the coast, Boston and Toronto and Philly, a bunch of Montreal Anglos and some wannabes in upstate New York, around Buffalo and Schenectady. I was doing Tribal work in London, serving the Eastern Standard Agenda, working with a couple of Tribesmen, well, one Tribesman and my girlfriend, who I thought was unaffiliated. Turns out, though, that they're both double agents. They sold out to the Pacific Daylight Tribe, lameass phonies out in LA, slick Silicon Valley bizdev sharks, pseudo hipsters in San Franscarcity. Once I threatened to expose them, they set me up, had me thrown in here."

I looked around proudly, having just completed a real fun little excursion through a topic near and dear to my heart. Mount Rushmore looked back at me, stony and bovine and uncomprehending.

"Baby," Lucy said, rolling her eyes again, "you need some new meds."

"Could be," I said. "But this is for real. Is there a comm on the ward? We can look it up together."

"Oh, *that*'ll prove it, all right. Nothing but truth online."

"I didn't say that. There're peer-reviewed articles about the Tribes. It was a lead story on the CBC's social science site last year."

"Uh huh, sure. Right next to the sasquatch videos."

"I'm talking about the CBC, Lucy. Let's go look it up."

Lucy mimed taking an invisible comm out of her cleavage and prodding at it with an invisible stylus. She settled an invisible pair of spectacles on her nose and nodded sagely. "Oh yeah, sure, really interesting stuff."

I realized that I was arguing with a crazy person and turned to the doctor. "You must have read about the Tribes, right?"

The doctor acted as if he hadn't heard me. "That's just fascinating, Art. Thank you for sharing that. Now, here's a question I'd like you to think about, and maybe you can tell us the answer tomorrow: What are the ways that your friends—the ones you say betrayed you—used to show you how much they respected you and liked you? Think hard about this. I think you'll be surprised by the conclusions you come to."

"What's that supposed to mean?"

"Just what I said, Art. Think hard about how you and your friends interacted and you'll see that they really like you."

"Did you hear what I just said? Have you heard of the Tribes?"

"Sure, sure. But this isn't about the Tribes, Art. This is about you and—" he consulted his comm, "Fede and Linda. They care about you a great deal and they're terribly worried about you. You just think about it. Now," he said, recrossing his legs, "Fatima, you told us yesterday about your mother and I asked you to think about how *she* feels. Can you tell the group what you found out?"

But Fatima was off in med-land, eyes glazed and mouth hanging slack. Manuel nudged her with his toe, then, when she failed to stir, aimed a kick at her shin. The doctor held a hand out and grabbed Manuel's slippered toe. "That's all right, let's move on to Lucy."

I tuned out as Lucy began an elaborate and well-worn rant about her eating habits, prodded on by the doctor. The enormity of the situation was coming home to me. I couldn't win. If I averred that Fede and Linda were my boon companions, I'd still be found incompetent—after all, what competent person threatens his boon companions? If I stuck to my story, I'd be found incompetent, and medicated besides, like poor little Fatima, zombified by the psychoactive cocktail. Either way, I was stuck.

Stuck on the roof now, and it's getting very uncomfortable indeed. Stuck because I am officially incompetent and doomed and damned to indefinite rest on the ward. Stuck because every passing moment here is additional time for the hamsters to run their courses in my mind, piling regret on worry.

Stuck because as soon as I am discovered, I will be stupified by the meds, administered by stern and loving and thoroughly disappointed doctors. I still haven't managed to remember any of their names. They are interchangeable, well shod and endowed with badges on lanyards and soothing and implacable and entirely unappreciative of my rhetorical skills.

Stuck. The sheet-metal chimneys stand tall around the roof, unevenly distributed according to some inscrutable logic that could only be understood with the assistance of as-built drawings, blueprints, mechanical and structural engineering diagrams. Surely though, they are optimized to wick hot air out of the giant brick pile's guts and exhaust it.

I move to the one nearest the stairwell. It is tarred in place, its apron lined with a double row of cinderblocks that have pools of brackish water and cobwebs gathered in their holes. I stick my hand in the first and drag it off the apron. I repeat it.

Now the chimney is standing on its own, in the middle of a nonsensical cinderblock-henge. My hands are dripping with muck and grotendousness. I wipe them off on the pea gravel and then dry them on my boxer shorts, then hug the chimney and lean forward. It gives, slowly, slightly, and springs back. I give it a harder push, really give it my weight, but it won't budge. Belatedly, I realize that I'm standing on its apron, trying to lift myself along with the chimney.

I take a step back and lean way forward, try again. It's awkward, but I'm making progress, bent like an ell, pushing with my legs and lower back. I feel something pop around my sacrum, know that I'll regret this deeply when my back kacks out completely, but it'll be all for naught if I don't keep! on! pushing!

Then, suddenly, the chimney gives, its apron swinging up and hitting me in the knees so that I topple forward with it, smashing my chin on its hood. For a moment, I lie down atop it, like a stupefied lover, awestruck by my own inanity. The smell of blood rouses me. I tentatively reach my hand to my chin and feel the ragged edge of a cut there, opened from the tip and along my jawbone almost to my ear. The cut is too fresh to hurt, but it's bleeding freely and I know it'll sting like a bastard soon enough. I go to my knees and scream, then scream again as I rend open my chin further.

My knees and shins are grooved with deep, parallel cuts, gritted with gravel and grime. Standing hurts so much that I go back to my knees, holler again at the pain in my legs as I grind more gravel into my cuts, and again as I tear my face open some more. I end up fetal on my side, sticky with blood and weeping softly with an exquisite self-pity that is more than the cuts and bruises, more than the betrayal, more than the foreknowledge of punishment. I am weeping for myself, and my identity, and my smarts over happiness and the thought that I would indeed choose happiness over smarts any day.

Too damned smart for my own good.

"**I just don't** get it," Fede said.

Art tried to keep the exasperation out of his voice. "It's simple," he said. "It's like a car radio with a fast-forward button. You drive around on the MassPike, and your car automatically peers with nearby vehicles. It grabs the current song on someone else's stereo and streamloads it. You listen to it. If you don't hit the fast-forward button, the car starts grabbing everything it can from the peer, all the music on the stereo, and queues it up for continued play. Once that pool is exhausted, it queries your peer for a list of its peers—the cars that it's getting its music from—and sees if any of them are in range, and downloads from them. So, it's like you're exploring a taste-network, doing an automated, guided search through traffic for the car whose owner has collected the music you most want to listen to."

"But I hate your music—I don't want to listen to the stuff on your radio."

"Fine. That's what the fast-forward button is for. It skips to another car and starts streamloading off of its drive." Fede started to say something, and Art held up his hand. "And if you exhaust all the available cars, the system recycles, but asks its peers for files collected from other sources. You might hate the songs I downloaded from Al, but the songs I got from Bennie are right up your alley.

"The war-drivers backstop the whole system. They've got the biggest collections on the freeway, and they're the ones most likely to build carefully thought-out playlists. They've got entire genres—the whole history of the blues, say, from steel cylinders on—on their drives. So we encourage them. When you go through a paypoint—a toll booth—we debit you for the stuff that you didn't fast-forward, the stuff you listened to and kept. Unless, that is, you've got more than, say, 10,000 songs onboard. Then you go free. It's counterintuitive, I know, but just look at the numbers."

"OK, OK. A radio with a fast-forward button. I think I get it."

"But?"

"But who's going to want to use this? It's unpredictable. You've got no guarantee you'll get the songs you want to hear."

Art smiled. "Exactly!"

Fede gave him a go-on wave.

"Don't you see? That's the crack-cocaine part! It's the thrill of the chase! Nobody gets excited about beating traffic on a back road that's always empty. But get on the M-5 after a hard day at work and drive it at 100 km/h for two hours without once touching your brakes and it's like God's reached down and parted the Red Seas for you. You get a sense of *accomplishment!* Most of the time, your car stereo's gonna play the same junk you've always heard, just background sound, but sometimes, ah! Sometimes you'll hit a sweet spot and get the best tunes you've ever heard. If you put a rat in a cage with a lever that doesn't give food pellets, he'll push it once or twice and give up. Set the lever to always deliver food pellets and he'll push it when he gets hungry. Set it to *sometimes* deliver food pellets and he'll bang on it until he passes out!"

"Heh," Fede said. "Good rant."

"And?"

"And it's cool." Fede looked off into the middle distance a while. "Radio with a fast-forward button. That's great, actually. Amazing. Stupendous!" He snatched the axe head from its box on Art's desk and did a little war dance around the room, whooping. Art followed the dance from his ergonomic chair, swiveling around as the interface tchotchkes that branched from its undersides chittered to keep his various bones and muscles firmly supported.

His office was more like a three-fifths-scale model of a proper office, in Lilliputian London style, so the war dance was less impressive than it might have been with more room to express itself. "You like it, then," Art said, once Fede had run out of steam.

"I do, I do, I do!"

"Great."

"Great."

"So."

"Yes?"

"So what do we do with it? Should I write up a formal proposal and send it to Jersey? How much detail? Sketches? Code fragments? Want me to mock up the interface and the network model?"

Fede cocked an eyebrow at him. "What are you talking about?"

"Well, we give this to Jersey, they submit the proposal, they walk away with the contract, right? That's our job, right?"

"No, Art, that's not our job. Our job is to see to it that V/DT submits a bad proposal, not that Jersey submits a good one. This is big. We roll this together and it's bigger than MassPike. We can run this across every goddamned toll road in the world! Jersey's not paying for this—not yet, anyway—and someone should."

"You want to sell this to them?"

"Well, I want to sell this. Who to sell it to is another matter."

Art waved his hands confusedly. "You're joking, right?"

Fede crouched down beside Art and looked into his eyes. "No, Art, I am serious as a funeral here. This is big, and it's not in the scope of work that we signed up for. You and me, we can score big on this, but not by handing it over to those shitheads in Jersey and begging for a bonus."

"What are you talking about? Who else would pay for this?"

"You have to ask? V/DT for starters. Anyone working

on a bid for MassPike, or TollPass, or FastPass, or EuroPass."

"But we can't sell this to just *anyone*, Fede!"

"Why not?"

"Jesus. Why not? Because of the Tribes."

Fede quirked him half a smile. "Sure, the Tribes."

"What does that mean?"

"Art, you know that stuff is four-fifths horseshit, right? It's just a game. When it comes down to your personal welfare, you can't depend on time zones. This is more job than calling, you know."

Art squirmed and flushed. "Lots of us take this stuff seriously, Fede. It's not just a mind-game. Doesn't loyalty mean anything to you?"

Fede laughed nastily. "Loyalty! If you're doing all of this out of loyalty, then why are you drawing a paycheck? Look, I'd rather that this go to Jersey. They're basically decent sorts, and I've drawn a lot of pay from them over the years, but they haven't paid for this. They wouldn't give us a free ride, so why should we give them one? All I'm saying is, we can offer this to Jersey, of course, but they have to bid for it in a competitive marketplace. I don't want to gouge them, just collect a fair market price for our goods."

"You're saying you don't feel any fundamental loyalty to anything, Fede?"

"That's what I'm saying."

"And you're saying that I'm a sucker for putting loyalty ahead of personal gain—after all, no one else is, right?"

"Exactly."

"Then how did this idea become 'ours,' Fede? I came up with it."

Fede lost his nasty smile. "There's loyalty and then there's loyalty."

"Uh-huh."

"No, really. You and I are a team. I rely on you and you rely on me. We're loyal to something concrete—each other. The Eastern Standard Tribe is an abstraction. It's a whole bunch of people, and neither of us like most of 'em. It's useful and pleasant, but you can't put your trust in institutions—otherwise you get Nazism."

"And patriotism."

"Blind patriotism."

"So there's no other kind? Just jingoism? You're either loyal to your immediate circle of friends or you're a deluded dupe?"

"No, that's not what I'm saying."

"So where does informed loyalty leave off and jingoism begin? You come on all patronizing when I talk about being loyal to the Tribe, and you're certainly not loyal to V/DT, nor are you loyal to Jersey. What greater purpose are you loyal to?"

"Well, humanity, for starters."

"Really. What's that when it's at home?"

"Huh?"

"How do you express loyalty to something as big and abstract as 'humanity'?"

"Well, that comes down to morals, right? Not doing

things that poison the world. Paying taxes. Change to panhandlers. Supporting charities." Fede drummed his fingers on his thighs. "Not murdering or raping, you know. Being a good person. A moral person."

"OK, that's a good code of conduct. I'm all for not murdering and raping, and not just because it's *wrong*, but because a world where the social norms include murdering and raping is a bad one for me to live in."

"Exactly."

"That's the purpose of morals and loyalty, right? To create social norms that produce a world you want to live in."

"Right! And that's why *personal* loyalty is important."

Art smiled. Trap baited and sprung. "OK. So institutional loyalty—loyalty to a Tribe or a nation—that's not an important social norm. As far as you're concerned, we could abandon all pretense of institutional loyalty." Art dropped his voice. "You could go to work for the Jersey boys, sabotaging Virgin/Deutsche Telekom, just because they're willing to pay you to do it. Nothing to do with Tribal loyalty, just a job."

Fede looked uncomfortable, sensing the impending rhetorical headlock. He nodded cautiously.

"Which means that the Jersey boys have no reason to be loyal to you. It's just a job. So if there were an opportunity for them to gain some personal advantage by selling you out, turning you into a patsy for them, well, they should just go ahead and do it, right?"

"Uh—"

"Don't worry, it's a rhetorical question. Jersey boys sell you out. You take their fall, they benefit. If there was no institutional loyalty, that's where you'd end up, right? That's the social norm you want."

"No, of course it isn't."

"No, of course not. You want a social norm where individuals can be disloyal to the collective, but not vice versa."

"Yes—"

"Yes, but loyalty is bidirectional. There's no basis on which you may expect loyalty from an institution unless you're loyal to it."

"I suppose."

"You know it. I know it. Institutional loyalty is every bit as much about informed self-interest as personal loyalty is. The Tribe takes care of me, I take care of the Tribe. We'll negotiate a separate payment from Jersey for this—after all, this is outside of the scope of work that we're being paid for—and we'll split the money, down the middle. We'll work in a residual income with Jersey, too, because, as you say, this is bigger than MassPike. It's a genuinely good idea, and there's enough to go around. All right?"

"Are you asking me or telling me?"

"I'm asking you. This will require both of our cooperation. I'm going to need to manufacture an excuse to go stateside to explain this to them and supervise the prototyping. You're going to have to hold down the fort here at V/DT and make sure that I'm clear to do my thing. If you want to go and sell this idea elsewhere, well, that's going to require my cooperation, or at least my silence—if I turn this over to V/DT, they'll pop you for industrial espionage. So we need each other."

Art stood and looked down at Fede, who was a good ten centimeters shorter than he, looked down at Fede's sweaty upper lip and creased brow. "We're a good team, Fede. I don't want to toss away an opportunity, but I also don't want to exploit it at the expense of my own morals. Can you agree to work with me on this, and trust me to do the right thing?"

Fede looked up. "Yes," he said. On later reflection, Art thought that the *yes* came too quickly, but then, he was just relieved to hear it. "Of course. Of course. Yes. Let's do it."

"That's just fine," Art said. "Let's get to work, then."

They fell into their traditional division of labor then, Art working on a variety of user-experience plans, dividing each into subplans, then devising protocols for user testing to see what would work in the field; Fede working on logistics from plane tickets to personal days to budget and critical-path charts. They worked side by side, but still used the collaboration tools that Art had grown up with, designed to allow remote, pseudonymous parties to fit their separate work components into the same structure, resolving schedule and planning collisions where it could and throwing exceptions where it couldn't. They worked beside each other and each hardly knew the other was there, and that, Art thought, when he thought of it, when the receptionist commed him to tell him that "Linderrr"—freakin' teabags—was there for him, that was the defining characteristic of a Tribalist. A norm, a modus operandi, a way of being that did not distinguish between communication face-to-face and communication at a distance.

"Linderrr?" Fede said, cocking an eyebrow.

"I hit her with my car," Art said.

"Ah," Fede said. "Smooth."

Art waved a hand impatiently at him and went out to the reception area to fetch her. The receptionist had precious little patience for entertaining personal visitors, and Linda, in track pants and a baggy sweater, was clearly not a professional contact. The receptionist glared at him as he commed into the lobby and extended his hand to Linda, who took it, put it on her shoulder, grabbed his ass, crushed their pelvises together and jammed her tongue in his ear. "I missed you," she slurped, the buzz of her voice making him writhe. "I'm not wearing any knickers," she continued, loud enough that he was sure that the receptionist heard. He felt the blush creeping over his face and neck and ears.

The receptionist. Dammit, why was he thinking about the receptionist? "Linda," he said, pulling away. Introduce her, he thought. Introduce them, and that'll make it less socially awkward. The English can't abide social awkwardness. "Linda, meet—" and he trailed off, realizing he didn't actually know the receptionist's name.

The receptionist glared at him from under a cap of shining candy-apple red hair, narrowing her eyes, which were painted in high style with Kubrick action-figure faces.

"My *name* is Tonaishah," she hissed. Or maybe it was *Tanya Iseah*, or *Taneesha*. He still didn't know her goddamned name.

"And this is Linda," he said, weakly. "We're going out tonight."

"And won't you have a dirty great time, then?" Tonaishah said.

"I'm sure we will," he said.

"Yes," Tonaishah said.

Art commed the door and missed the handle, then snagged it and grabbed Linda's hand and yanked her through.

"I'm a little randy," she said, directly into his ear. "Sorry." She giggled.

"Someone you have to meet," he said, reaching down to rearrange his pants to hide his boner.

"Ooh, right here in your office?" Linda said, covering his hand with hers.

"Someone with *two* eyes," he said, moving her hand to his hip.

"Ahh," she said. "What a disappointment."

"I'm serious. I want you to meet my friend Fede. I think you two will really hit it off."

"Wait," Linda said. "Isn't this a major step? Meeting the friends? Are we getting that serious already?"

"Oh, I think we're ready for it," Art said, draping an arm around her shoulders and resting his fingertips on the upper swell of her breast.

She ducked out from under his arm and stopped in her tracks. "Well, I don't. Don't I get a say in this?"

"What?" Art said.

"Whether it's time for me to meet your friends or not. Shouldn't I have a say?"

"Linda, I just wanted to introduce you to a coworker before we went out. He's in my office—I gotta grab my jacket there, anyway."

"Wait, is he a friend or a coworker?"

"He's a friend I work with. Come on, what's the big deal?"

"Well, first you spring this on me, then you change your story and tell me he's a coworker, now he's a friend again. I don't want to be put on display for your pals. If we're going to meet your friends, I'll dress for it, put on some makeup. This isn't fair."

"Linda," Art said, placating.

"No," she said. "Screw it. I'm not here to meet your friends. I came all the way across town to meet you at your office because you wanted to head back to your place after work, and you play headgames with me like this?"

"All right," Art said. "I'll show you back out to the lobby and you can wait with Tonaishah while I get my jacket."

"Don't take that tone with me," she said.

"What tone?" Art said. "Jesus Christ! You can't wait in the hall, it's against policy. You don't have a badge, so you have to be with me or in the lobby. I don't give a shit if you meet Fede or not."

"I won't tell you again, Art," she said. "Moderate your tone. I won't be shouted at."

Art tried to rewind the conversation and figure out how they came to this pass, but he couldn't. Was Linda really acting *this* nuts? Or was he just reading her wrong or pushing her buttons or something?

"Let's start over," he said, grabbing both of her hands in his. "I need to get my jacket from my office. You can come with me if you want to, and meet my friend Fede. Otherwise you can wait in the lobby, I won't be a minute."

"Let's go meet Fede," she said. "I hope he wasn't expecting anything special, I'm not really dressed for it."

He stifled a snotty remark. After all that, she was going to go and meet Fede? So what the hell were they arguing about? On the other hand, he'd gotten his way, hadn't he? He led her by the hand to his office, and beyond every doorway they passed was a V/DT Experience Designer pretending not to peek at them as they walked by, having heard every word through the tricky acoustics of O'Malley House.

"Fede," he said, stiffly, "This is Linda. Linda, this is Fede."

Fede stood and treated Linda to his big, suave grin.

Fede might be short and he might have paranoid delusions, but he was trim and well groomed, with the sort of finicky moustache that looked like a rotting caterpillar if you didn't trim it every morning. He liked to work out, and had a tight waist and a gut you could bounce a quarter off of, and liked to wear tight shirts that showed off his overall fitness, made him stand out among the spongy mouse-potatoes of the corporate world. Art had never given it much thought, but now, standing with Fede and Linda in his tiny office, breathing in Fede's Lilac Vegetal and Linda's new-car-smell shampoo, he felt paunchy and sloppy.

"Ah," Fede said, taking her hand. "The one you hit with your car. It's a pleasure. You seem to be recovering nicely, too."

Linda smiled and gave him a peck on the cheek, a few strands of her bobbed hair sticking to his moustache like cobwebs as she pulled away.

"It was just a love tap," she said. "I'll be fine."

"Fede's from New York," Art said. "We colonials like to stick together around the office. And Linda's from Los Angeles."

"Aren't there any, you know, British people in London?" Linda said, wrinkling her nose.

"There's Tonaishah," Art said weakly.

"Who?" Fede said.

"The receptionist," Linda said. "Not a very nice person."

"With the eyes?" Fede said, wriggling his fingers

around his temples to indicate elaborate eye makeup.

"That's her," Linda said.

"Nasty piece of work," Fede said. "Never trusted her."

"*You're* not another UE person, are you?" Linda said, sizing Fede up and giving Art a playful elbow in the ribs.

"Who, me? Nah. I'm a management consultant. I work in Chelsea mostly, but when I come slumming in Piccadilly, I like to comandeer Art's office. He's not bad, for a UE-geek."

"Not bad at all," Linda said, slipping an arm around Art's waist, wrapping her fingers around the waistband of his trousers. "Did you need to grab your jacket, honey?"

Art's jacket was hanging on the back of his office door, and to get at it, he had to crush himself against Linda and maneuver the door shut. He felt her breasts soft on his chest, felt her breath tickle his ear, and forgot all about their argument in the corridor.

"All right," Art said, hooking his jacket over his shoulder with a finger, feeling flushed and fluttery. "OK, let's go."

"Lovely to have met you, Fede," Linda said, taking his hand.

"And likewise," Fede said.

>>>>>>>>>>15

Vigorous sex ensued.

>>>>>>>>>>16

Art rolled out of bed at dark o'clock in the morning, awakened by circadians and endorphins and bladder. He staggered to the toilet in the familiar gloom of his shabby little rooms, did his business, marveled at the tenderness of his privates, fumbled for the flush mechanism—"British" and "plumbing" being two completely opposite notions—and staggered back to bed. The screen of his comm, nestled on the end table, washed the room in liquid-crystal light. He'd tugged the sheets off of Linda when he got up, and there she was, chest rising and falling softly, body rumpled and sprawled after their gymnastics. It had been transcendent and messy, and the sheets were coarse with dried fluids.

He knelt on the bed and fussed with the covers some, trying for an equitable—if not chivalrously so—division of blankets. He bent forward to kiss at a bite mark he'd left on her shoulder.

His back went *pop*.

Somewhere down in the lumbar, somewhere just above his tailbone, a deep and unforgiving *pop*, ominous as the cocking of a revolver. He put his hand there and it felt OK, so he cautiously lay back. Three-quarters of the way down, his entire lower back seized up, needles of fire raced down his legs and through his groin, and he collapsed.

He *barked* with pain, an inhuman sound he hadn't known he could make, and the rapid emptying of his lungs deepened the spasm, and he mewled. Linda opened a groggy eye and put her hand on his shoulder. "What is it, hon?"

He tried to straighten out, to find a position in which the horrible, relentless pain returned whence it came. Each motion was agony. Finally, the pain subsided, and he found himself pretzelled, knees up, body twisted to the left, head twisted to the right. He did not dare budge from this posture, terrified that the pain would return.

"It's my back," he gasped.

"Whah? Your back?"

"I—I put it out. Haven't done it in years. I need an icepack, OK? There're some headache pills in the medicine cabinet. Three of those."

"Seriously?"

"Look, I'd get 'em myself, but I can't even sit up,

much less walk. I gotta ice this down now before it gets too inflamed."

"How did it happen?"

"It just happens. Tai Chi helps. Please, I need ice."

Half an hour later, he had gingerly arranged himself with his knees up and his hips straight, and he was breathing deeply, willing the spasms to unclench. "Thanks," he said.

"What now? Should I call a doctor?"

"He'd just give me painkillers and tell me to lose some weight. I'll probably be like this for a week. Shit. Fede's going to kill me. I was supposed to go to Boston next Friday, too."

"Boston? What for? For how long?"

Art bunched the sheets in his fists. He hadn't meant to tell her about Boston yet—he and Fede hadn't worked out his cover story. "Meetings," he said. "Two or three days. I was going to take some personal time and go see my family, too. Goddamnit. Pass me my comm, OK?"

"You're going to *work* now?"

"I'm just going to send Fede a message and send out for some muscle relaxants. There's a twenty-four-hour chemist's at Paddington Station that delivers."

"I'll do it, you lie flat."

And so it began. Bad enough to be helpless, weak as a kitten and immobile, but to be at the whim of someone else, to have to provide sufficient excuse for every use of his comm, every crawl across the flat . . . Christ.

"Just give me my comm, please. I can do it faster than I can explain how to do it."

In thirty-six hours, he was ready to tear the throat out of anyone who tried to communicate with him. He'd harangued Linda out of the flat and crawled to the kitchen floor, painstakingly assembling a nest of pillows and sofa cushions, close to the icemaker and the painkillers and toilet. His landlady, an unfriendly Chinese lady who had apparently been wealthy beyond words in Hong Kong and clearly resented her reduced station, agreed to sign for the supply drops he commed to various retailers around London.

He was giving himself a serious crick in his neck and shoulder from working supine, comm held over his head. The painkillers weighted his arms and churned his guts, and at least twice an hour, he'd grog his way into a better position, forgetting the tenderness in his back, and bark afresh as his nerves shrieked and sizzled.

Two days later and he was almost unrecognizable, a gamey, unshaven lump in the tiny kitchen, his nest gray with sweat and stiff with spilled take-away curry. He suspected that he was overmedicating, forgetting whether he'd taken his tablets and taking more. In one of his more lucid moments, he realized that there was a feedback cycle at play here—the more pills he took, the less equipped he was to judge whether he'd taken his pills, so the more pills he took. His mind meandered through a solution to this, a timer-equipped pillcase that reset when you took the lid off and chimed if you took the lid off again before the set interval had elapsed. He reached for his comm to make some notes, found it wedged under one of his hocks, greasy with sweat, batteries dead. He hadn't let his comm run down in a decade, at least.

His landlady let Linda in on the fourth day, as he was sleeping fitfully with a pillow over his face to shut out the light from the window. He'd tried to draw the curtains a day—two days?—before, but had given up when he tried to pull himself upright on the sill only to collapse in a fresh gout of writhing. Linda crouched by his head and stroked his greasy hair softly until he flipped the pillow off his face with a movement of his neck. He squinted up at her, impossibly fresh and put together and incongruous in his world of reduced circumstances.

"Art. Art. Art. Art! You're a mess, Art! Jesus. Why aren't you in bed?"

"Too far," he mumbled.

"What would your grandmother say? Dear-oh-dearie. Come on, let's get you up and into bed, and then I'm going to have a doctor and a massage therapist sent in. You need a nice, hot bath, too. It'll be good for you and hygienic besides."

"No tub," he said petulantly.

"I know, I know. Don't worry about it. I'll sort it out."

And she did, easing him to his feet and helping him into bed. She took his house keys and disappeared for some unknowable time, then reappeared with fresh linen in store wrappers, which she lay on the bed carefully, making tight hospital corners and rolling him over, nurse-style, to do the other side. He heard her clattering in the kitchen, running the faucets, moving furniture. He reminded himself to ask her to drop his comm in its charger, then forgot.

"Come on, time to get up again," she said, gently peeling the sheets back.

"It's OK," he said, waving weakly at her.

"Yes, it is. Let's get up." She took his ankles and gradually turned him on the bed so that his feet were on the floor, then grabbed him by his stinking armpits and helped him to his feet. He stumbled with her into his crowded living room, dimly aware of the furniture stacked on itself around him. She left him hanging on the door lintel and then began removing his clothes. She actually used a scissors to cut away his stained tee shirt and boxer shorts. "All right," she said, "into the tub."

"No tub," he said.

"Look down, Art," she said.

He did. An inflatable wading pool sat in the middle of his living room, flanked by an upended coffee table and his sofa, standing on its ear. The pool was full of steaming, cloudy water. "There's a bunch of eucalyptus oil and Epsom salts in there. You're gonna love it."

That night, Art actually tottered into the kitchen and got himself a glass of water, one hand pressed on his lower back. The cool air of the apartment fanned the mentholated liniment on his back and puckered goose pimples all over his body. After days of leaden limbs, he felt light and clean, his senses singing as though he was emerging from a fever. He drank the water, and retrieved his comm from its cradle.

He propped several pillows up on his headboard and fired up his comm. Immediately, it began to buzz and hum and chatter and blink, throwing up alerts about urgent messages, pages and calls pending. The lightness he'd felt fled him, and he began the rotten business of triaging his in-box.

One strong impression emerged almost immediately: Fede wanted him in Boston.

The Jersey clients were interested in the teasers that Fede had forwarded to them. The Jersey clients were obsessed with the teasers that Fede had forwarded to them. The Jersey clients were howling for more after the teasers that Fede had forwarded to them. Fede had negotiated some big bucks on approval if only Art would go and talk to the Jersey clients. The Jersey clients had arranged a meeting with some of the MassPike decision-makers for the following week, and now they were panicking because they didn't have anything *except* the teasers Fede had forwarded to them.

You should really try to go to Boston, Art. We need you in Boston, Art. You have to go to Boston, Art. Art, go to Boston. Boston, Art. Boston.

Linda rolled over in bed and peered up at him. "You're *not* working again, are you?"

"Shhh," Art said. "It's less stressful if I get stuff done than if I let it pile up."

"Then why is your forehead all wrinkled up?"

"I have to go to Boston," he said. "Day after tomorrow, I think."

"Jesus, are you insane? Trying to cripple yourself?"

"I can recover in a hotel room just as well as I can recover here. It's just rest from here on in, anyway. And a hotel will probably have a tub."

"I can't believe I'm hearing this. You're not going to *recover* in Boston. You'll be at meetings and stuff. Christ!"

"I've got to do this," Art said. "I just need to figure out how. I'll go business class, take along a lumbar pillow, and spend every moment that I'm not in a meeting in a tub or getting a massage. I could use a change of scenery about now, anyway."

"You're a goddamned idiot, you know that?"

Art knew it. He also knew that here was an opportunity to get back to EST, to make a good impression on the Jersey clients, to make his name in the Tribe and to make a bundle of cash. His back be damned, he was sick of lying around anyway. "I've got to go, Linda."

"It's your life," she said, and tossed aside the covers. "But I don't have to sit around watching you ruin it." She disappeared into the hallway, then reemerged, dressed and with her coat on. "I'm out of here."

"Linda," Art said.

"No," she said. "Shut up. Why the fuck should I

care if you don't, huh? I'm going. See you around."

"Come on, let's talk about this."

East-Coast pizza. Flat Boston twangs. The coeds rushing through Harvard Square and oh, maybe a side trip to New York, maybe another up to Toronto and a roti at one of the halal Guyanese places on Queen Street. He levered himself painfully out of bed and hobbled to the living room, where Linda was arguing with a taxi dispatcher over her comm, trying to get them to send out a cab at two in the morning.

"Come on," Art said. "Hang that up. Let's talk about this."

She shot him a dirty look and turned her back, kept on ranting down the comm at the dispatcher.

"Linda, don't do this. Come on."

"I am on the phone!" she said to him, covering the mouthpiece. "Shut the fuck up, will you?" She uncovered the mouthpiece. "Hello? Hello?" The dispatcher had hung up. She snapped the comm shut and slammed it into her purse. She whirled to face Art, snorting angry breaths through her nostrils. Her face was such a mask of rage that Art recoiled, and his back twinged. He clasped at it and carefully lowered himself onto the sofa.

"Don't do this, OK?" he said. "I need support, not haranguing."

"What's there to say? Your mind's already made up. You're going to go off and be a fucking idiot and cripple yourself. Go ahead, you don't need my permission."

"Sit down, please, Linda, and talk to me. Let me explain my plan and my reasons, OK? Then I'll listen to you. Maybe we can sort this out and actually, you know, come to understand each other's point of view."

"Fine," she said, and slammed herself into the sofa. Art bounced and he seized his back reflexively, waiting for the pain, but beyond a low-grade throbbing, he was OK.

"I have a very large opportunity in Boston right now. One that could really change my life. Money, sure, but prestige and profile, too. A dream of an opportunity. I need to attend one or two meetings, and then I can take a couple days off. I'll get Fede to OK a first-class flight—we get chits we can use to upgrade to Virgin Upper; they've got hot tubs and massage therapists now. I'll check into a spa—they've got a bunch on Route 128—and get a massage every morning and have a physiotherapist up to the room every night. I can't afford that stuff here, but Fede'll spring for it if I go to Boston, let me expense it. I'll be a good lad, I promise."

"I still think you're being an idiot. Why can't Fede go?"

"Because it's my deal."

"Why can't whoever you're meeting with come here?"

"That's complicated."

"Bullshit. I thought you wanted to talk about this?"

"I do. I just can't talk about that part."

"Why not? Are you afraid I'll blab? Christ, Art. Give me some credit. Who the hell would I blab *to*, anyway?"

"Look, Linda, the deal itself is confidential—a secret. A secret's only a secret if you don't tell it to anyone, all right? So I'm not going to tell you. It's not relevant to the discussion, anyway."

"Art. Art. Art. Art, you make it all sound so reasonable, and you can dress it up with whatever words you want, but at the end of the day, we both know you're full of shit on this. There's no *way* that doing this is better for you than staying here in bed. If Fede's the problem, let me talk to him."

"Jesus, no!"

"Why not?"

"It's not appropriate, Linda. This is a work-related issue. It wouldn't be professional. OK, I'll concede that flying and going to meetings is more stressful than not flying and not going to meetings, but let's take it as a given that I *really* need to go to Boston. Can't we agree on that, and then discuss the ways that we can mitigate the risks associated with the trip?"

"Jesus, you're an idiot," she said, but she seemed to be on the verge of smiling.

"But I'm your idiot, right?" Art said, hopefully.

"Sure, sure you are." She *did* smile then, and cuddle up to him on the sofa. "They don't have fucking *hot tubs* in Virgin Upper, do they?"

"Yeah," Art said, kissing her earlobe. "They really do."

Once the blood coursing from my shins slows and clots, I take an opportunity to inspect the damage more closely. The cuts are relatively shallow, certainly less serious than they were in my runamuck imagination, which had vivid slashes of white bone visible through the divided skin. I cautiously pick out the larger grit and gravel and turn my attention spinewards.

I have done a number on my back, that much is certain. My old friends, the sacroiliac joints, feel as tight as drumheads, and they creak ominously when I shift to a sitting position with my back propped up on the chimney's upended butt, the aluminum skirting cool as a kiss on my skin. They're only just starting to twinge, a hint of the agonies to come.

My jaw, though, is pretty bad. My whole face feels swollen, and if I open my mouth the blood starts anew.

You know, on sober reflection, I believe that coming up to the roof was a really bad idea.

I use the chimney to lever myself upright again, and circle it to see exactly what kind of damage I've done. There's a neat circular hole in the roof where the chimney used to be, gusting warm air into my face as I peer into its depths. The hole is the mouth of a piece of shiny metal conduit about the circumference of a basketball hoop. When I put my head into it, I hear the white noise of a fan, somewhere below in the building's attic. I toss some gravel down the conduit and listen to the report as it *pings* off the fan blades down below. That's a good, loud sound, and one that is certain to echo through the building.

I rain gravel down the exhaust tube by the handful, getting into a mindless, shuffling rhythm, wearing the sides of my hands raw and red as I scrape the pebbles up into handy piles. Soon I am shuffling afield of the fallen chimney, one hand on my lumbar, crouched over like a chimp, knees splayed in an effort to shift stress away from my grooved calves.

I'm really beating the shit out of that poor fan, I can tell. The shooting-gallery rattle of the gravel ricocheting off the blades is dulling now, sometimes followed by secondary rattles as the pebbles bounce back into the blades. Not sure what I'll do if the fan gives out before someone notices me up here.

It's not an issue, as it turns out. The heavy fire door beyond the chimney swings open abruptly. A hospital maintenance gal in coveralls, roly-poly and draped with tool belts and bandoliers. She's red-faced from the trek up the stairs, and it gives her the aspect of a fairy-tale baker or candy-seller. She reinforces this impression by putting her plump hands to her enormous bosom and gasping when she catches sight of me.

It comes to me that I am quite a fucking sight. Bloody, sunburnt, wild-eyed, with my simian hunch and my scabby jaw set at a crazy angle to my face and reality both. Not to mention my near nudity, which I'm semipositive is not her idea of light entertainment. "Hey," I say. "I, uh, I got stuck on the roof. The door shut." Talking reopens the wound on my jaw and I feel more blood trickling down my neck. "Unfortunately, I only get one chance to make a first impression, huh? I'm not, you know, really *crazy*, I was just a little bored and so I went exploring and got stuck and tried to get someone's attention, had a couple accidents . . . It's a long story. Hey! My name's Art. What's yours?"

"Oh my Lord!" she said, and her hand jumps to the hammer in its bandolier holster on her round tummy. She claws at it frantically.

"Please," I say, holding my hands in front of me. "Please. I'm hurt is all. I came up here to get some fresh air and the door swung shut behind me. I tripped when I knocked over the chimney to get someone's attention. I'm not dangerous. Please. Just help me get back down to the twentieth floor—I think I might need a stretcher crew, my back is pretty bad."

"It's Caitlin," she says.

"I beg your pardon?"

"My name is Caitlin," she says.

"Hi, Caitlin," I said. I extend my hand, but she doesn't move the ten yards she would have to cross in order to take it. I think about moving towards her, but think better of it.

"You're not up here to jump, are you?"

"Jump? Christ, no! Just stuck is all. Just stuck."

Linda's goddamned boyfriend was into all this flaky Getting to Yes shit, subliminal means of establishing rapport and so on. Linda and I once spent an afternoon at the Children's Carousel uptown in Manhattan, making fun of all his newage theories. The one that stood out in my mind as funniest was synching your breathing—"What you resist persists, so you need to turn resistance into assistance," Linda recounted. You match breathing with your subject for fifteen breaths and they unconsciously become receptive to your suggestions. I have a suspicion that Caitlin might bolt, duck back through the door and pound down the stairs on her chubby little legs and leave me stranded.

So I try it, match my breath to her heaving bosom. She's still panting from her trek up the stairs and fifteen breaths go by in a quick pause. The silence stretches, and I try to remember what I'm supposed to do next. Lead the subject, that's it. I slow my breathing down gradually and, amazingly, her breath slows down along with mine, until we're both breathing great, slow breaths. It works—it's flaky and goofy California shit, but it works.

"Caitlin," I say calmly, making it part of an exhalation.

"Yes," she says, still wary.

"Have you got a comm?"

"I do, yes."

"Can you please call downstairs and ask them to send up a stretcher crew? I've hurt my back and I won't be able to handle the stairs."

"I can do that, yes."

"Thank you, Caitlin."

It feels like cheating. I didn't have to browbeat her or puncture her bad reasoning—all it took was a little rapport, a little putting myself in her shoes. I can't believe it worked, but Caitlin flips a ruggedized comm off her hip and speaks into it in a calm, efficient manner.

"Thank you, Caitlin," I say again. I start to ease myself to a sitting position, and my back gives way, so that I crash to the rooftop, mewling, hands clutched to my spasming lumbar. And then Caitlin's at my side, pushing my hands away from my back, strong thumbs digging into the spasming muscles around my sacroiliac, soothing and smoothing them out, tracing the lines of fire back to the nodes of the joints, patiently kneading the spasms out until the pain recedes to a soft throbbing.

"My old man used to get that," she said. "All us kids had to take turns working it out for him." I'm on my back, staring up over her curves and rolls and into her earnest, freckled face.

"Oh, God, that feels good," I say.

"That's what the old man used to say. You're too young to have a bad back."

"I have to agree," I say.

"All right, I'm going to prop your knees up and

lay your head down. I need to have a look at that ventilator."

I grimace. "I'm afraid I did a real number on it," I say. "Sorry about that."

She waves a chubby pish-tosh at me with her freckled hand and walks over to the chimney, leaving me staring at the sky, knees bent, waiting for the stretcher crew.

When they arrive, Caitlin watches as they strap me onto the board, tying me tighter than is strictly necessary for my safety, and I realize that I'm not being tied *down*, I'm being tied *up*.

"Thanks, Caitlin," I say.

"You're welcome, Art."

"Good luck with the ventilator—sorry again."

"That's all right, kid. It's my job, after all."

>>>>>>>>>>18

Virgin Upper's hot tubs were more theoretically soothing than actually so. They had rather high walls and a rather low water level, both for modesty's sake and to prevent spills. Art passed through the miniature sauna/shower and into the tub after his massage, somewhere over Newfoundland, and just as the plane hit turbulence, buffeting him with chlorinated water that stung his eyes and got up his nose and soaked the magazine on offshore investing that he'd found in the back of his seat pocket.

He landed at JFK still smelling of chlorine and sandalwood massage oil and the cantaloupe-scented lotion in the fancy toilets. Tension melted away from him as he meandered to the shuttle stop. The air had an indefinable character of homeliness, or maybe it was the sunlight. Amateur Tribal anthropologists were always thrashing about light among themselves, arguing about the sun's character varying from latitude to latitude, filtered through this city's pollution signature or that.

The light or the air, the latitude or the smog, it felt like home. The women walked with a reassuring, confident *clack clack clack* of heel on hard tile; the men talked louder than was necessary to one another or to their comms. The people were a riot of ethnicities and their speech was a riotous babel of accents, idioms and languages. Aggressive pretzel vendors vied with aggressive panhandlers to shake down the people waiting on the shuttle bus. Art bought a stale, sterno-reeking pretzel that was crusted with inedible volumes of yellowing salt and squirted a couple bucks at a panhandler who had been pestering him in thick Jamaican patois but thanked him in adenoidal Brooklynese.

By the time he boarded his connection to Logan he was joggling his knees uncontrollably in his seat, his delight barely contained. He got an undrinkable can of watery Budweiser and propped it up on his tray table alongside his inedible pretzel and arranged them in a kind of symbolic tableau of all things ESTian.

He commed Fede from the guts of the tunnels that honeycombed Boston, realizing with a thrill as Fede picked up that it was two in the morning in London, at the nominal GMT+0, while here at GMT-5—at the default, plus-zero time zone of his life, livelihood and lifestyle—it was only 9PM.

"Fede!" Art said into the comm.

"Hey, Art!" Fede said, with a false air of chipperness that Art recognized from any number of middle-of-the-night calls.

There was a cheap Malaysian comm that he'd once bought because of its hyped up de-hibernate feature—its ability to go from its deepest power-saving sleepmode to full waking glory without the customary thirty seconds of drive-churning housekeeping as it reestablished its network connection, verified its file system and memory, and pinged its buddy list for state and presence info. This Malaysian comm, the Crackler, had the uncanny ability to go into suspended animation indefinitely, and yet throw your workspace back on its display in a hot instant.

When Art actually laid hands on it, after it meandered its way across the world by slow boat, corrupt GMT+8 Posts and Telegraphs authorities, over-engineered courier services and Revenue Canada's Customs agents, he was enchanted by this feature. He could put the device into deep sleep, close it up, and pop its cover open and *poof!* there were his windows. It took him three days and an interesting crash to notice that even though he was seeing his workspace, he wasn't able to interact with it for thirty seconds. The auspicious crash revealed the presence of a screenshot of his pre-hibernation workspace on the drive, and he realized that the machine was tricking him, displaying the screenshot—the illusion of wakefulness—when he woke it up, relying on the illusion to endure while it performed its housekeeping tasks in the background. A little stopwatch work proved that this chicanery actually added three seconds to the overall wake-time, and taught him his first important user-experience lesson: perception of functionality trumps the actual function.

And here was Fede, throwing up a verbal screenshot of wakefulness while he churned in the background, housekeeping himself into real alertness. "Fede, I'm here, I'm in Boston!"

"Good Art, good. How was the trip?"

"Wonderful. Virgin Upper was fantastic—dancing girls, midget wrestling, hash brownies . . ."

"Good, very good."

"And now I'm driving around under Boston through a land-yacht regatta. The boats are mambo, but I think that banana patch the hotel soon."

"Glad to hear it." Art heard water running dimly, realized that Fede was taking a leak.

"Meeting with the Jersey boys tomorrow. We're having brunch at a strip club."

"OK, OK, very funny," Fede said. "I'm awake. What's up?"

"Nothing. I just wanted to check in with you and let you know I arrived safe and sound. How're things in London?"

"Your girlfriend called me."

"Linda?"

"You got another girlfriend?"

"What did she want?"

"She wanted to chew me out for sending you overseas with your 'crippling back injury.' She told me she'd hold me responsible if you got into trouble over there."

"God, Fede, I'm sorry. I didn't put her up to it or anything—"

"Don't worry about it. I'm glad that there's someone out there who cares about you. We're getting together for dinner tonight."

"Fede, you know, I think Linda's terrific, but she's a little, you know, volatile."

"Art, everyone in O'Malley House knows just how volatile she is. 'I won't tell you again, Art. Moderate your tone. I won't be shouted at.'"

"Christ, you heard that, too?"

"Don't worry about it. She's cool and I like her and I can stand to be shouted at a little. When did you say you were meeting with Perceptronics?"

The word shocked him. They never mentioned the name of the Jersey clients. It started as a game, but soon became woven into Fede's paranoid procedures.

Now they had reached the endgame. Within a matter of weeks, they'd be turning in their resignations to V/DT and taking the final flight across the Atlantic and back to GMT-5, provocateurs no longer.

"Tomorrow afternoon. We're starting late to give me time to get a full night's sleep." The last conference call with Perceptronics had gone fantastically. His normal handlers—sour men with nasty minds who glommed onto irrelevancies in V/DT's strategy and teased at them until they conjured up shadowy and shrewd conspiracies where none existed— weren't on that call. Instead, he'd spent a rollicking four hours on the line with the sharp and snarky product designers and engineers, bouncing ideas back and forth at speed. Even over the phone, the homey voices and points of view felt indefinably comfortable and familiar. They'd been delighted to start late in the day for his benefit, and had offered to work late and follow up with a visit to a bar where he could get a burger the size of a baby's head. "We're meeting at Perceptronics's branch office in Acton tomorrow and the day after, then going into MassPike. The Perceptronics guys sound really excited." Just saying the name of the company was a thrill.

"That's really excellent, Art. Go easy, though—"

"Oh, don't worry about me. My back's feeling miles better." And it was, loose and supple the way it did after a good workout.

"That's good, but it's not what I meant. We're still closing this deal, still dickering over price. I need another day, maybe, to settle it. So go easy tomorrow. Give me a little leverage, OK?"

"I don't get it. I thought we had a deal."

"Nothing's final till it's vinyl, you know that. They're balking at the royalty clause—" Fede was proposing to sell Perceptronics an exclusive license on the business-model patent he'd filed for using Art's notes in exchange for jobs, a lump-sum payment and a royalty on every sublicense that Perceptronics sold to the world's toll roads. "—and we're renegotiating. They're just playing hardball, is all. Another day, tops, and I'll have it sorted."

"I'm confused. What do you want me to do?"

"Just, you know, *stall* them. Get there late. Play up your jetlag. Leave early. Don't get anything, you know, *done*. Use your imagination."

"Is there a deal or isn't there, Fede?"

"There's a deal, there's a deal. I'll do my thing, you'll do your thing, and we'll both be rich and living in New York before you know it. Do you understand?"

"Not really."

"OK, that'll have to be good enough for now. Jesus, Art, I'm doing my best here, all right?"

"Say hi to Linda for me, OK?"

"Don't be pissed at me, Art."

"I'm not pissed. I'll stall them. You do your thing. I'll take it easy, rest up my back."

"All right. Have a great time, OK?"

"I will, Fede."

Art rang off, feeling exhausted and aggravated. He followed the tunnel signs to the nearest up-ramp, wanting to get into the sunlight and architecture and warm himself with both. A minuscule BMW Flea blatted its horn at him when he changed lanes. Had he cut the car off? He was still looking the wrong way, still anticipating oncoming traffic on the right. He raised a hand in an apologetic wave.

It wasn't enough for the Flea's driver. The car ran right up to his bumper, then zipped into the adjacent lane, accelerated and cut him off, nearly causing a wreck. As it was, Art had to swerve into the parking lane on Mass Ave—how did he get to Mass Ave? God, he was lost already—to avoid him. The Flea backed off and switched lanes again, then pulled up alongside of him. The driver rolled down his window.

"How the fuck do you like it, jackoff? Don't *ever* fucking cut me off!" He was a middle-aged white guy in a suit, driving a car that was worth a year's wages to Art, purple-faced and pop-eyed.

Art felt something give way inside, and then he was shouting back. "When I want your opinion, I'll squeeze your fucking head, you sack of shit! As it is, I can barely contain my rage at the thought that a scumbag like you is consuming *air* that the rest of us could be breathing! Now, roll up your goddamned window and drive your fucking bourge-mobile before I smash your fucking head in!"

He shut his mouth, alarmed. What the hell was he

saying? How did he end up standing here, outside of his car, shouting at the other driver, stalking towards the Flea with his hands balled into fists? Why was he picking a fight with this goddamned psycho, anyway? A year in peaceful, pistol-free London had eased his normal road-rage defense systems. Now they came up full, and he wondered if the road-rager he'd just snapped at would haul out a Second-Amendment Special and cap him.

But the other driver looked as shocked as Art felt. He rolled up his window and sped off, turning wildly at the next corner—Brookline, Art saw. Art got back into his rental, pulled off to the curb and asked his comm to generate an optimal route to his hotel, and drove in numb silence the rest of the way.

>>>>>>>>>>19

They let me call Gran on my second day here. Of course, Linda had already called her and briefed her on my supposed mental breakdown. I had no doubt that she'd managed to fake hysterical anxiety well enough to convince Gran that I'd lost it completely; Gran was already four-fifths certain that I was nuts.

"Hi, Gran," I said.

"Arthur! My God, how are you?"

"I'm fine, Gran. It's a big mistake is all."

"A mistake? Your lady friend called me and told me what you'd done in London. Arthur, you need help."

"What did Linda say?"

"She said that you threatened to kill a coworker. She said you threatened to kill *her*. That you had a knife. Oh, Arthur, I'm so worried—"

"It's not true, Gran. She's lying to you."

"She told me you'd say that."

"Of course she did. She and Fede—a guy I worked with in London—they're trying to get rid of me. They had me locked up. I had a business deal with Fede, we were selling one of my ideas to a company in New Jersey. Linda talked him into selling to some people she knows in LA instead, and they conspired to cut me out of the deal. When I caught them at it, they got me sent away. Let me guess, she told you I was going to say this, too, right?"

"Arthur, I know—"

"You know that I'm a good guy. You raised me. I'm not nuts, OK? They just wanted to get me out of the way while they did their deal. A week or two and I'll be out again, but it will be too late. Do you believe that you know me better than some girl I met a month ago?"

"Of *course* I do, Arthur. But why would the hospital take you away if—"

"If I wasn't crazy? I'm in here for observation— they want to find *out* if I'm crazy. If *they're* not sure, then you can't be sure, right?"

"All right. Oh, I've been sick with worry."

"I'm sorry, Gran. I need to get through this week and I'll be free and clear and I'll come back to Toronto."

"I'm going to come down there to see you. Linda told me visitors weren't allowed, is that true?"

"No, it's not true." I thought about Gran seeing me in the ward amidst the pukers and the screamers and the droolers and the *fondlers* and flinched away from the phone. "But if you're going to come down, come for the hearing at the end of the week. There's nothing you can do here now."

"Even if I can't help, I just want to come and see you. It was so nice when you were here."

"I know, I know. I'll be coming back soon, don't worry."

If only Gran could see me now, on the infirmary examination table, in four-point restraint. Good thing she can't.

A doctor looms over me. "How are you feeling, Art?"

"I've had better days," I say, with what I hope is stark sanity and humor. Aren't crazy people incapable of humor? "I went for a walk and the door swung shut behind me."

"Well, they'll do that," the doctor says. "My name is Szandor," he says, and shakes my hand in its restraint.

"A pleasure to meet you," I say. "You're a *doctor* doctor, aren't you?"

"An MD? Yup. There're a couple of us around the place."

"But you're not a shrink of any description?"

"Nope. How'd you guess?"

"Bedside manner. You didn't patronize me."

Dr. Szandor tries to suppress a grin, then gives up. "We all do our bit," he says. "How'd you get up on the roof without setting off your room alarm, anyway?"

"If I tell you how I did it, I won't be able to repeat the trick," I say jokingly. He's swabbing down my shins now with something that stings and cools at the same time. From time to time, he takes tweezers in hand and plucks loose some gravel or grit and plinks it into a steel tray on a rolling table by his side. He's so gentle, I hardly feel it.

"What, you never heard of doctor-patient confidentiality?"

"Is that thing still around?"

"Oh sure! We had a mandatory workshop on it yesterday afternoon. Those are always a lot of fun."

"So, you're saying that you've got professional expertise in the keeping of secrets, huh? I suppose I could spill it for you, then." And I do, explaining my little hack for tricking the door into thinking that I'd left and returned to the room.

"Huh—now that you explain it, it's pretty obvious."

"That's my job—figuring out the obvious way of doing something."

And we fall to talking about my job with V/DT, and the discussion branches into the theory and practice of UE, only slowing a little when he picks the crud out of the scrape down my jaw and tugs through a couple of quick stitches. It occurs to me that he's just keeping me distracted, using a highly evolved skill for placating psychopaths through small talk so that they don't thrash while he's knitting their bodies back together.

I decide that I don't care. I get to natter on about a subject that I'm nearly autistically fixated on, and I do it in a context where I know that I'm sane and smart and charming and occasionally mind-blowing.

". . . and the whole thing pays for itself through EZPass, where we collect the payments for the music downloaded while you're on the road." As I finish my spiel, I realize *I've* been keeping *him* distracted, standing there with the tweezers in one hand and a swab in the other.

"Wow!" he said. "So, when's this all going to happen?"

"You'd use it, huh?"

"Hell, yeah! I've got a good twenty, thirty thousand on my car right now! You're saying I could plunder anyone else's stereo at will, for free, and keep it, while I'm stuck in traffic, and because I'm a—what'd you call it, a super-peer?—a super-peer, it's all free and legal? Damn!"

"Well, it may be a while before you see it on the East Coast. It'll probably roll out in LA first, then San Francisco, Seattle . . . "

"What? Why?"

"It's a long story," I say. "And it ends with me on the roof of a goddamned nuthouse on Route 128 doing a one-man tribute to the Three Stooges."

Three days later, Art finally realized that something big and ugly was in the offing. Fede had repeatedly talked him out of going to Perceptronics's offices, offering increasingly flimsy excuses and distracting him by calling the hotel's front desk and sending up surprise massage therapists to interrupt Art as he stewed in his juices, throbbing with resentment at having been flown thousands of klicks while injured in order to check into a faceless hotel on a faceless stretch of highway and insert this thumb into his asshole and wait for Fede—*who was still in fucking London!*—to sort out the mess so that he could present himself at the Perceptronics Acton offices and get their guys prepped for the ever-receding meeting with MassPike.

"Jesus, Federico, what the fuck am I *doing* here?"

"I know, Art, I know." Art had taken to calling Fede at the extreme ends of circadian compatibility, three AM and eleven PM and then noon on Fede's clock, as a subtle means of making the experience just as unpleasant for Fede as it was for Art. "I screwed up," Fede yawned. "I screwed up and now we're both paying the price. You handled your end beautifully and I dropped mine. And I intend to make it up to you."

"I don't *want* more massages, Fede. I want to get this shit done and I want to come home and see my girlfriend."

Fede tittered over the phone.

"What's so funny?"

"Nothing much," Fede said. "Just sit tight there for a couple minutes, OK? Call me back once it happens and tell me what you wanna do, all right?"

"Once what happens?"

"You'll know."

It was Linda, of course. Knocking on Art's hotel room door minutes later, throwing her arms—and then her legs—around him, and banging him stupid, half on and half off the hotel room bed. Riding him and then being ridden in turns, slurping and wet and energetic until they both lay sprawled on the hotel room's very nice Persian rugs, dehydrated and panting and Art commed Fede, and Fede told him it could take a couple weeks to sort things out, and why didn't he and Linda rent a car and do some sight-seeing on the East Coast?

That's exactly what they did. Starting in Boston, where they cruised Cambridge, watching the cute nerdyboys and geekygirls wander the streets, having heated technical debates, lugging half-finished works of technology and art through the sopping summertime, a riot of townie accents and highbrow engineerspeak.

Then a week in New York, where they walked until they thought their feet would give out entirely, necks cricked at a permanent, upward-staring angle to gawp at the topless towers of Manhattan. The sound the sound the sound of Manhattan rang in their ears, a gray and deep rumble of cars and footfalls and subways and steampipes and sirens and music and conversation and ring tones and hucksters and schizophrenic ranters, a veritable Las Vegas of cacophony, and it made Linda uncomfortable, she who was raised in the white-noise susurrations of LA's freeway forests, but it made Art feel *wonderful*. He kept his comm switched off, though the underfoot rumble of the subway had him reaching for it a hundred times a day, convinced that he'd left it on in vibe-alert mode.

They took a milk-run train to Toronto, chuffing through sleepy upstate New York towns, past lakes and rolling countryside in full summer glory. Art and Linda drank ginger beer in the observation car, spiking it with rum from a flask that Linda carried in a garter that she wore for the express purpose of being able to reach naughtily up her little sundress and produce a bottle of body-temperature liquor in a nickel-plated vessel whose shiny sides were dulled by the soft oil of her thigh.

Canada Customs and Immigration separated them at the border, sending Art for a full inspection—a privilege of being a Canadian citizen and hence perennially under suspicion of smuggling goods from the tax havens of the US into the country—and leaving Linda in their little Pullman cabin.

When Art popped free of the bureaucracy, his life

thoroughly peered into, he found Linda standing on the platform, leaning against a pillar, back arched, one foot flat against the bricks, corresponding dimpled knee exposed to the restless winds of the trainyard. From Art's point of view, she was a gleaming vision skewered on a beam of late-day sunlight that made her hair gleam like licorice. Her long and lazy jaw caught and lost the sun as she talked animatedly down her comm, and Art was struck with a sudden need to sneak up behind her and run his tongue down the line that began with the knob of her mandible under her ear and ran down to the tiny half-dimple in her chin, to skate it on the soft pouch of flesh under her chin, to end with a tasting of her soft lips.

Thought became deed. He crept up on her, smelling her new-car hair products on the breeze that wafted back from her, and was about to begin his tonguing when she barked, "Fuck *off!* Stop calling me!" and closed her comm and stormed off trainwards, leaving Art standing on the opposite side of the pillar with a thoroughly wilted romantic urge.

More carefully, he followed her into the train, back to their little cabin, and reached for the palm-pad to open the door when he heard her agitated comm voice. "No, goddamnit, no. Not yet. Keep calling me and not *ever*, do you understand?"

Art opened the door. Linda was composed and neat and sweet in her plush seat, shoulders back, smile winning. "Hey, honey, did the bad Customs man finally let you go?"

"He did! That sounded like a doozy of a phone conversation, though. What's wrong?"

"You don't want to know," she said.

"All right," Art said, sitting down opposite her, knee-to-knee, bending forward to plant a kiss on the top of her exposed thigh. "I don't."

"Good."

He continued to kiss his way up her thigh. "Only . . ."

"Yes?"

"I think I probably do. Curiosity is one of my worst failings of character."

"Really?"

"Quite so," he said. He'd slid her sundress right up to the waistband of her cotton drawers, and now he worried one of the pubic hairs that poked out from the elastic with his teeth.

She shrieked and pushed him away. "Someone will see!" she said. "This is a border crossing, not a bordello!"

He sat back, but inserted a finger in the elastic before Linda straightened out her dress, so that his fingertip rested in the crease at the top of her groin.

"You are *naughty*," she said.

"And curious," Art agreed, giving his fingertip a playful wiggle.

"I give up. That was my fucking ex," she said. "That is how I will refer to him henceforth. 'My fucking ex.' My fucking, pain-in-the-ass, touchy-feely ex. My fucking ex, who wants to have the Talk, even though it's been months and months. He's figured out that I'm stateside from my calling times, and he's offering to come out to meet me and really Work Things Out, Once And For All."

"Oh, my," Art said.

"That boy's got too much LA in him for his own good. There's no problem that can't be resolved through sufficient dialog."

"We never really talked about him," Art said.

"Nope, we sure didn't."

"Did you want to talk about him now, Linda?"

"'Did you want to talk about him now, Linda?' Why yes, Art, I would. How perceptive of you." She pushed his hand away and crossed her arms and legs simultaneously.

"Wait, I'm confused," Art said. "Does that mean you want to talk about him, or that you don't?"

"Fine, we'll talk about him. What do you want to know about my fucking ex?"

Art resisted a terrible urge to fan her fires, to return the vitriol that dripped from her voice. "Look, you don't want to talk about him, we won't talk about him," he managed.

"No, let's talk about my fucking ex, by all means." She adopted a singsong tone and started ticking off points on her fingers. "His name is Toby, he's half-Japanese, half-white. He's about your height. Your dick is bigger, but he's better in bed. He's a user-experience designer at Lucas-SGI, in Studio City. He never fucking shuts up about what's wrong with this or that. We dated for two years, lived together for one year, and broke up just before you and I met. I broke it off with him: He was making me goddamned crazy and he wanted me to come back from London and live with him. I wanted to stay out the year in England and go back to my own apartment and possibly a different boyfriend, and he made me choose, so I chose. Is that enough of a briefing for you, Arthur?"

"That was fine," Art said. Linda's face had gone rabid purple, madly pinched, spittle flecking off of her lips as she spat out the words. "Thank you."

She took his hands and kissed the knuckles of his thumbs. "Look, I don't like to talk about it—it's painful. I'm sorry he's ruining our holiday. I just won't take his calls anymore, how about that?"

"I don't care, Linda, honestly, I don't give a rat's ass if you want to chat with your ex. I just saw how upset you were and I thought it might help if you could talk it over with me."

"I know, baby, I know. But I just need to work some things out all on my own. Maybe I will take a quick trip out west and talk things over with him. You could come if you want—there are some wicked bars in West Hollywood."

"That's OK," Art said, whipsawed by Linda's incomprehensible mood shifts. "But if you need to go, go. I've got plenty of old pals to hang out with in Toronto."

"You're so understanding," she cooed. "Tell me about your grandmother again—you're sure she'll like me?"

"She'll love you. She loves anything that's female, of childbearing years, and in my company. She has great and unrealistic hopes of great-grandchildren."

"Cluck."

"Cluck?"

"Just practicing my brood-hen."

>>>>>>>>>>21

Doc Szandor's a good egg. He's keeping the shrinks at bay, spending more time with me than is strictly necessary. I hope he isn't neglecting his patients, but it's been so long since I had a normal conversation, I just can't bear to give it up. Besides, I get the impression that Szandor's in a similar pit of bad conversation with psychopaths and psychothera-pists and is relieved to have a bit of a natter with someone who isn't either having hallucinations or attempting to prevent them in others.

"How the hell do you become a User-Experience guy?"

"Sheer orneriness," I say, grinning. "I was just in the right place at the right time. I had a pal in New

York who was working for a biotech company that had made this artificial erectile tissue."

"Erectile tissue?"

"Yeah. Synthetic turtle penis. Small and pliable and capable of going large and rigid very quickly."

"Sounds delightful."

"Oh, it was actually pretty cool. You know the joke about the circumcisionist's wallet made from fore-skins?"

"Sure, I heard it premed—he rubs it and it becomes a suitcase, right?"

"That's the one. So these guys were thinking about making drawbridges, temporary shelters, that kind of thing out of it. They even had a cute name for it: 'Ardorite.'"

"Ho ho ho."

"Yeah. So they weren't shipping a whole lot of product, to put it mildly. Then I spent a couple of weeks in Manhattan housesitting for my friend while he was visiting his folks in Wisconsin for Thanksgiving. He had a ton of this stuff lying around his apartment, and I would come back after walking the soles off my shoes and sit in front of the tube playing with it. I took some of it down to Madison Square Park and played with it there. I liked to hang out there because it was always full of these very cute Icelandic au pairs and their tots, and I was a respectable enough young man with about 200 words of Icelandic I'd learned from a friend's mom in high school and they thought I was adorable and I thought they were blond goddesses. I'd gotten to be friends with one named Marta, oh, Marta. Bookmark Marta, Szandor, and I'll come back to her once we're better acquainted.

"Anyway, Marta was in charge of Machinery and Avarice, the spoiled monsterkinder of a couple of BBD&O senior managers who'd vaulted from art school to VPdom in one year when most of the gray eminences got power-thraxed. Machinery was three and liked to bang things against other things arythmically while hollering atonally. Avarice was five, not toilet trained, and prone to tripping. I'd get Marta novelty coffee from the Stinkbucks on Twenty-third and we'd drink it together while Machinery and Avarice engaged in terrible, life-threatening play with the other kids in the park.

"I showed Marta what I had, though I was tactful enough not to call it *synthetic turtle penis*, because while Marta was earthy, she wasn't *that* earthy and, truth be told, it got me kinda hot to watch her long, pale blue fingers fondling the soft tissue, then triggering the circuit that hardened it.

"Then Machinery comes over and snatches the thing away from Marta and starts pounding on Avarice, taking unholy glee in the way the stuff alternately softened and stiffened as he squeezed it. Avarice wrestled it away from him and tore off for a knot of kids and by the time I got there they were all crowded around her, spellbound. I caught a cab back to my buddy's apartment and grabbed all the Ardorite

I could lay hands on and brought it back to the park and spent the next couple hours running an impromptu focus group, watching the kids and their bombshell nannies play with it. By the time that Marta touched my hand with her long cool fingers and told me it was time for her to get the kids home for their nap, I had twenty-five toy ideas, about eight different ways to use the stuff for clothing fasteners, and a couple of miscellaneous utility uses, like a portable crib.

"So I ran it down for my pal that afternoon over the phone, and he commed his boss and I ended up eating Thanksgiving dinner at his boss's house in Westchester."

"Weren't you worried he'd rip off your ideas and not pay you anything for them?" Szandor's spellbound by the story, unconsciously unrolling and re-rolling an Ace bandage.

"Didn't even cross my mind. Of course, he tried to do just that, but it wasn't any good—they were engineers; they had no idea how normal human beings interact with their environments. The stuff wasn't self-revealing—they added a million cool features and a manual an inch thick. After prototyping for six months, they called me in and offered me a two-percent royalty on any products I designed for them."

"That musta been worth a fortune," says Szandor.

"You'd think so, wouldn't you? Actually, they folded before they shipped anything. Blew through all their capital on R&D, didn't have anything left to productize their tech with. But my buddy *did* get another gig with a company that was working on new kitchen stuff made from one-way osmotic materials and he showed them the stuff I'd done with the Ardorite and all of a sudden I had a no-fooling career."

"Damn, that's cool."

"You betcha. It's all about being an advocate for the user. I observe what users do and how they do it, figure out what they're trying to do, and then boss the engineers around, getting them to remove the barriers they've erected because engineers are all basically high-functioning autistics who have no idea how normal people do stuff."

The doctor chuckles. "Look," he says, producing a nicotine pacifier, one of those fake cigs that gives you the oral fix and the chemical fix and the habit fix without the noxious smoke, "it's not my area of specialty, but you seem like a basically sane individual, modulo your rooftop adventures. Certainly, you're not like most of the people we've got here. What are you doing here?"

Doctor Szandor is young, younger even than me, I realize. Maybe twenty-six. I can see some fancy tattoo-work poking out of the collar of his shirt, see some telltale remnant of a fashionable haircut in his grown-out shag. He's got to be the youngest staff member I've met here, and he's got a fundamentally different affect from the zombies in the lab coats who maintain the zombies in the felt slippers.

So I tell him my story, the highlights, anyway. The

more I tell him about Linda and Fede, the dumber my own actions sound to me.

"Why the hell did you stick with this Linda anyway?" Szandor says, sucking on his pacifier.

"The usual reasons, I guess," I say, squirming.

"Lemme tell you something," he says. He's got his feet up on the table now, hands laced behind his neck. "It's the smartest thing my dad ever said to me, just as my high-school girl and me were breaking up before I went away to med school. She was nice enough, but, you know, *unstable*. I'd gotten to the point where I ducked and ran for cover every time she disagreed with me, ready for her to lose her shit.

"So my dad took me aside, put his arm around me, and said, 'Szandor, you know I like that girlfriend of yours, but she is crazy. Not a little crazy, really crazy. Maybe she won't be crazy forever, but if she gets better, it won't be because of you. Trust me, I know this. You can't fuck a crazy girl sane, son.'"

I can't help smiling. "Truer words," I say. "But harsh."

"Harsh is relative," he says. "Contrast it with, say, getting someone committed on trumped-up evidence."

It dawns on me that Doc Szandor believes me. "It dawns on me that you believe me."

He gnaws fitfully at his pacifier. "Well, why not? You're not any crazier than I am, that much is clear to me. You have neat ideas. Your story's plausible enough."

I get excited. "Is this your *professional* opinion?"

"Sorry, no. I am not a mental health professional, so I don't have professional opinions on your mental health. It is, however, my amateur opinion."

"Oh, well."

"So where are you at now, vis-à-vis the hospital?"

"Well, they don't tell me much, but as near as I can make out, I am stuck here semipermanently. The court found me incompetent and ordered me held until I was. I can't get anyone to explain what competency consists of, or how I achieve it—when I try, I get accused of being 'difficult.' Of course, escaping onto the roof is a little beyond difficult. I have a feeling I'm going to be in pretty deep shit. Do they know about the car?"

"The car?"

"In the parking lot. The one that blew up."

Doc Szandor laughs hard enough that his pacifier shoots across the room and lands in a hazmat bucket. "You son of a bitch—that was you?"

"Yeah," I say, and drum my feet against the tin cupboards under the examination table.

"That was *my fucking car!*"

"Oh, Christ, I'm sorry," I say. "God."

"No no no," he says, fishing in his pocket and unwrapping a fresh pacifier. "It's OK. Insurance. I'm getting a bike. Vroom, vroom! What a coincidence, though," he says.

Coincidence. He's making disgusting hamster-cage noises, grinding away at his pacifier. "Szandor, do you

sometimes sneak out onto the landing to have a cigarette? Use a bit of tinfoil for your ashtray? Prop the
door open behind you?"

"Why do you ask?"

"'Cause that's how I got out onto the roof."

"Oh, shit," he says.

"It's our secret," I say. "I can tell them I don't know
how I got out. I'm incompetent, remember?"

"You're a good egg, Art," he says. "How the hell are
we going to get you out of here?"

"Hey, what?"

"No, really. There's no good reason for you to be
here, right? You're occupying valuable bed space."

"Well, I appreciate the sentiment, but I have a feeling that as soon as you turn me loose, I'm gonna be
doped up to the tits for a good long while."

He grimaces. "Right, right. They like their meds.
Are your parents alive?"

"What? No, they're both dead."

"Aha. Died suddenly?"

"Yeah. Dad drowned, Mom fell—"

"Ah ah ah! Shhh. Mom died suddenly. She was taking Haldol when it happened, a low antianxiety dose,
right?"

"Huh?"

"Probably she was. Probably she had a terrible drug
interaction. Sudden Death Syndrome. It's hereditary.
And you say she fell? Seizure. We'll sign you up for a
PET scan, that'll take at least a month to set up. You
could be an epileptic and not even know it. Shaking

the radioisotopes loose for the scan from the AEC, whoa, that's a week's worth of paperwork right there! No Thorazine for you young man, not until we're absolutely sure it won't kill you dead where you stand. The hospital counsel gave us all a very stern lecture on this very subject not a month ago. I'll just make some notes in your medical history." He picked up his comm and scribbled.

"Never woulda thought of that," I say. "I'm impressed."

"It's something I've been playing with for a while now. I think that psychiatric care is a good thing, of course, but it could be better implemented. Taking away prescription pads would be a good start."

"Or you could keep public stats on which doctors had prescribed how much of what and how often. Put 'em on a chart in the ward where the patients' families could see 'em."

"That's *nasty!*" he says. "I love it. We're supposed to be accountable, right? What else?"

"Give the patients a good reason to wear their tracking bracelets: redesign them so they gather stats on mobility and vitals and track them against your meds and other therapies. Create a dating service that automatically links patients who respond similarly to therapies so they can compare notes. Ooh, by comparing with location data from other trackers, you could get stats on which therapies make people more sociable, just by counting the frequency with which patients stop and spend time in proximity to other patients. It'd give you empirical data with which you track your own progress."

"This is great stuff. Damn! How do you do that?"

I feel a familiar swelling of pride. I like it when people understand how good I am at my job. Working at V/DT was hard on my ego: after all, my job there was to do a perfectly rotten job, to design the worst user experiences that plausibility would allow. God, did I really do that for two whole goddamned years?

"It's my job," I say, and give a modest shrug.

"What do you charge for work like that?"

"Why, are you in the market?"

"Who knows? Maybe after I figure out how to spring you, we can go into biz together, redesigning nuthatches."

>>>>>>>>>>22

Linda's first meeting with Art's Gran went off without a hitch. Gran met them at Union Station with an obsolete redcap who was as ancient as she was, a vestige of a more genteel era of train travel and bulky luggage. Just seeing him made Art's brain whir with plans for conveyor systems, luggage escalators, cart

dispensers. They barely had enough luggage between
the two of them to make it worth the old man's time,
but he dutifully marked their bags with a stub of
chalk and hauled them onto his cart, then trundled
off to the service elevators.

Gran gave Art a long and teary hug. She was less
frail than she'd been in his memory, taller and stur-
dier. The smell of her powder and the familiar acoustics of Union Station's cavernous platform whirled
him back to his childhood in Toronto, to the homey
time before he'd gotten on the circadian merry-go-
round.

"Gran, this is Linda," he said.

"Oh, it's so *nice* to meet you," Gran said, taking
Linda's hands in hers. "Call me Julie."

Linda smiled a great, pretty, toothy smile. "Julie,
Art's told me all about you. I just *know* we'll be great
friends."

"I'm sure we will. Are you hungry? Did they feed you
on the train? You must be exhausted after such a long
trip. Which would you rather do first, eat or rest?"

"Well, *I'm* up for seeing the town," Linda said. "Your
grandson's been yawning his head off since Buffalo,
though." She put her arm around his waist and
squeezed his tummy.

"What a fantastic couple you make," Gran said.
"You didn't tell me she was so *pretty*, Arthur!"

"Here it comes," Art said. "She's going to ask about
great-grandchildren."

"Don't be silly," Gran said, cuffing him gently upside the head. "You're always exaggerating."

"Well *I* think it's a splendid idea," Linda said. "Shall we have two? Three? Four?"

"Make it ten," Art said, kissing her cheek.

"Oh, I couldn't have ten," Linda said. "But five is a nice compromise. Five it will be. We'll name the first one Julie if it's a girl, or Julius if it's a boy."

"Oh, we *are* going to get along," Gran said, and led them up to the curb, where the redcap had loaded their bags into a cab.

They ate dinner at Lindy's on Yonge Street, right in the middle of the sleaze strip. The steakhouse had been there for the better part of a century, and its cracked red-vinyl booths and thick rib eyes smothered in horseradish and HP Sauce were just as Art had remembered. Riding up Yonge Street, the city lights had seemed charming and understated; even the porn marquees felt restrained after a week in New York. Art ate a steak as big as his head and fell into a postprandial torpor whence he emerged only briefly to essay a satisfied belch. Meanwhile, Gran and Linda nattered away like old friends, making plans for the week: the zoo, the island, a day trip to Niagara Falls, a ride up the CN Tower, all the touristy stuff that Art had last done in elementary school.

By the time Art lay down in his bed, belly tight with undigested steak, he was feeling wonderful and at peace with the world. Linda climbed in beside him, wrestled away a pillow and some covers, and snuggled up to him.

"That went well," Art said. "I'm really glad you two hit it off."

"Me too, honey," Linda said, kissing his shoulder through his tee shirt. He'd been able to get his head around the idea of sharing a bed with his girlfriend under his grandmother's roof, but doing so nude seemed somehow wrong.

"We're going to have a great week," he said. "I wish it would never end."

"Yeah," she said, and began to snore into his neck.

The next morning, Art woke stiff and serene. He stretched out on the bed, dimly noted Linda's absence, and padded to the bathroom to relieve his bladder. He thought about crawling back into bed, was on the verge of doing so, when he heard the familiar, nervewracking harangue of Linda arguing down her comm. He opened the door to his old bedroom and there she was, stark naked and beautiful in the morning sun, comm in hand, eyes focused in the middle distance, shouting.

"No, goddamnit, no! Not here. Jesus, are you a moron? I said *no!*"

Art reached out to touch her back, noticed that it was trembling, visibly tense and rigid, and pulled his hand back. Instead, he quietly set about fishing in his small bag for a change of clothes.

"This is *not* a good time. I'm at Art's grandmother's place, all right? I'll talk to you later." She threw her comm at the bed and whirled around.

"Everything all right?" Art said timidly.

"No, goddamnit, no it isn't."

Art pulled on his pants and kept his eyes on her comm, which was dented and scratched from a hundred thousand angry hang ups. He hated it when she got like this, radiating anger and spoiling for a fight.

"I'm going to have to go, I think," she said.

"Go?"

"To California. That was my fucking ex again. I need to go and sort things out with him."

"Your ex knows who I am?"

She looked blank.

"You told him you were at my grandmother's place. He knows who I am?"

"Yeah," she said. "He does. I told him, so he'd get off my back."

"And you have to go to California?"

"Today. I have to go to California today."

"Jesus, today? We just got here!"

"Look, you've got lots of catching up to do with your Gran and your friends here. You won't even miss me. I'll go for a couple days and then come back."

"If you gotta go," he said.

"I gotta go."

He explained things as best as he could to Gran while Linda repacked her backpack, and then saw Linda off in a taxi. She was already savaging her comm, booking a ticket to LA. He called Fede from the condo's driveway.

"Hey, Art! How's Toronto?"

"How'd you know I was in Toronto?" Art said, but he knew, he *knew* then, though he couldn't explain how he knew, he knew that Linda and Fede had been talking. He *knew* that Linda had been talking to Fede that morning, and not her fucking ex (God, he was thinking of the poor schmuck that way already, "fucking ex"). Christ, it was *five in the morning* on the West Coast. It couldn't be the ex. He just knew.

"Lucky guess," Fede said breezily. "How is it?"

"Oh, terrific. Great to see the old hometown and all. How're things with Perceptronics? When should I plan on being back in Boston?"

"Oh, it's going all right, but slow. Hurry up and wait, right? Look, don't worry about it, just relax there, I'll call you when the deal's ready and you'll go back to Boston and we'll sort it out and it'll all be fantastic and don't worry, really, all right?"

"Fine, Fede." Art wasn't listening any more. Fede had gone into bullshit mode, and all Art was thinking of was why Linda would talk to Fede and then book a flight to LA. "How're things in London?" he said automatically.

"Fine, fine," Fede said, just as automatically. "Not the same without you, of course."

"Of course," Art said. "Well, bye then."

"Bye," Fede said.

Art felt an unsuspected cunning stirring within him. He commed Linda, in her cab. "Hey, dude," he said.

"Hey," she said, sounding harassed.

"Look, I just spoke to my Gran and she's really upset you had to go. She really liked you."

"Well, I liked her, too."

"Great. Here's the thing," he said, and drew in a breath. "Gran made you a sweater. She made me one, too. She's a knitter. She wanted me to send it along after you. It looks pretty good. So, if you give me your ex's address, I can FedEx it there and you can get it."

There was a lengthy pause. "Why don't I just pick it up when I see you again?" Linda said, finally.

Gotcha, Art thought. "Well, I know that'd be the *sensible* thing, but my Gran, I dunno, she really wants me to do this. It'd make her so happy."

"I dunno—my ex might cut it up or something."

"Oh, I'm sure he wouldn't do that. I could just schedule the delivery for after you arrive, that way you can sign for it. What do you think?"

"I really don't think—"

"Come on, Linda, I know it's nuts, but it's my Gran. She *really* likes you."

Linda sighed. "Let me comm you the address, OK?"

"Thanks, Linda," Art said, watching an address in Van Nuys scroll onto his comm's screen. "Thanks a bunch. Have a great trip—don't let your ex get you down."

Now, armed with Linda's fucking ex's name, Art went to work. He told Gran he had some administrative chores to catch up on for an hour or two, promised to have supper with her and Father Ferlenghetti

that night, and went out onto the condo's sundeck
with his keyboard Velcroed to his thigh.

Trepan: Hey!

Colonelonic: Trepan! Hey, what's up? I hear you're back on
the East Coast!

Trepan: True enough. Back in Toronto. How's things with
you?

Colonelonic: Same as ever. Trying to quit the dayjob.

Trepan: /private Colonelonic Are you still working at
Merrill-Lynch?

Colonelonic (private): Yeah.

Trepan: /private Colonelonic Still got access to Lexis-
Nexis?

Colonelonic (private): Sure——but they're on our asses
about abusing the accounts. Every search is logged
and has to be accounted for.

Trepan: /private Colonelonic Can you get me background on
just one guy?

Colonelonic (private): Who is he? Why?

Trepan: /private Colonelonic It's stupid. I think that
someone I know is about to go into biz with him, and
I don't trust him. I'm probably just being paranoid,
but . . .

Colonelonic (private): I don't know, man. Is it really
important?

Trepan: /private Colonelonic Oh, crap, look. It's my girlfriend. I think she's screwing this guy. I just wanna
get an idea of who he is, what he does, you know.

Colonelonic (private): Heh. That sucks. OK——check back

in a couple hours. There's a guy across the hall who
never logs out of his box when he goes to lunch. I'll
sneak in there and look it up on his machine.

Trepan: /private Colonelonic Kick ass. Thanks.

Transferring addressbook entry ''Toby Ginsburg'' to
Colonelonic. Receipt confirmed.

Trepan: /private Colonelonic Thanks again!

Colonelonic (private): Check in with me later——I'll
have something for you then.

Art logged off, flushed with triumph. Whatever
Fede and Linda were cooking up, he'd get wise to it
and then he'd nail 'em. What the hell was it, though?

>>>>>>>>>>**23**

My cousins visited me a week after I arrived at the nuthouse. I'd never been very close to them, and certainly our relationship had hardly blossomed during
the week I spent in Toronto, trying to track down
Linda and Fede's plot.

I have two cousins. They're my father's sister's kids,
and I didn't even meet them until I was about twenty
and tracking down my family history. They're Ottawa
Valley kids, raised on government-town pork, aging
hippie muesli, and country-style corn pone. It's a
weird mix, and we've never had a conversation that I

would consider a success. Ever met a violent, aggressive hippie with an intimate knowledge of whose genitals one must masticate in order to get a building permit or to make a pot bust vanish? It ain't pretty.

Cousin the first is Audie. She's a year older than me, and she's the smart one on that side of the family, the one who ended up at Queen's University for a BS in Electrical Engineering and an MA in Poli Sci, and even so finished up back in Ottawa, freelancing advice to clueless MPs dealing with Taiwanese and Sierra Leonese OEM importers. Audie's married to a nice fella whose name I can never remember and they're gonna have kids in five years; it's on a timetable that she actually showed me once when I went out there on biz and stopped in to see her at the office.

Cousin the second is Alphie—three years younger than me, raised in the shadow of his overachieving sister, he was the capo of Ottawa Valley script kiddies, a low-rent hacker who downloaded other people's code for defeating copyright protection and made a little biz for himself bootlegging games, porn, music and video, until the WIPO bots found him through traffic analysis and busted his ass, bankrupting him and landing him in the clink for sixty days.

Audie and Alphie are blond and ruddy and a little heavyset, all characteristics they got from their father's side, so add that to the fact that I grew up without being aware of their existence and you'll understand the absence of any real fellow-feeling for them. I don't dislike them, but I have so little in common with them that it's like hanging out with time travelers from the least-interesting historical era imaginable.

But they came to Boston and looked me up in the nuthatch.

They found me sitting on the sofa in the ward, post-Group, arms and ankles crossed, dozing in a shaft of sunlight. It was my habitual napping spot, and I found that a nap between Group and dinner was a good way to sharpen my appetite and anesthetize my taste buds, which made the mealtime slop bearable.

Audie shook my shoulder gently. I assumed at first that she was one of the inmates trying to get me involved in a game of Martian narco-checkers, so I brushed her hand away.

"They've probably got him all doped up," Audie said. The voice was familiar and unplaceable and so I cracked my eyelid, squinting up at her silhouette in the afternoon sun. "There he is," she said. "Come on, up and at 'em, tiger."

I sat up abruptly and scrubbed at my eyes. "Audie?" I asked.

"Yup. And Alphie." Alphie's pink face hove into view.

"Hi, Art," he mumbled.

"Jesus," I said, getting to my feet. Audie put out a superfluous steadying hand. "Wow."

"Surprised?" Audie said.

"Yeah!" I said. Audie thrust a bouquet of flowers into my arms. "What are you doing here?"

"Oh, your grandmother told me you were here. I was coming down to Boston for work anyway, so I flew in a day early so I could drop in. Alphie came down with me—he's my assistant now."

I almost said something about convicted felons working for government contractors, but I held onto my tongue. Consequently, an awkward silence blossomed.

"Well," Audie said, at last. "Well! Let's have a look at you, then." She actually took a lap around me, looking me up and down, making little noises. "You look all right, Art. Maybe a little skinny, even. Alphie's got a box of cookies for you." Alphie stepped forward and produced the box, a family pack of President's Choice Ridiculous Chocoholic Extra Chewies, a Canadian store brand I'd been raised on. Within seconds of seeing them, my mouth was sloshing with saliva.

"It's good to see you, Audie, Alphie." I managed to say it without spitting, an impressive feat, given the amount of saliva I was contending with. "Thanks for the care package."

We stared at each other blankly.

"So, Art," Alphie said, "So! How do you like it here?"

"Well, Alphie," I said. "I can't say as I do, really. As far as I can tell, I'm sane as I've ever been. It's just a bunch of unfortunate coincidences and bad judgment that got me here." I refrained from mentioning Alphie's propensity for lapses in judgment.

"Wow," Alphie said. "That's a bummer. We should do something, you know, Audie?"

"Not really my area of expertise," Audie said in clipped tones. "I would if I could, you know that, right Art? We're family, after all."

"Oh, sure," I say magnanimously. But now that I'm looking at them, my cousins who got into a thousand times more trouble than I ever did, driving drunk, pirating software, growing naughty smokables in the backyard, and got away from it unscathed, I feel a stirring of desperate hope. "Only . . ."

"Only what?" Alphie said.

"Only, maybe, Audie, do you think you could, that is, if you've got the time, do you think you could have a little look around and see if any of your contacts could maybe set me up with a decent lawyer who might be able to get my case reheard? Or a shrink, for that matter? Something? 'Cause frankly it doesn't really seem like they're going to let me go, ever. Ever."

Audie squirmed and glared at her brother. "I don't really know anyone that fits the bill," she said at last.

"Well, not *firsthand*, sure, why would you? You wouldn't." I thought that I was starting to babble, but I couldn't help myself. "You wouldn't. But maybe there's someone that someone you know knows who can do something about it? I mean, it can't hurt to ask around, can it?"

"I suppose it can't," she said.

"Wow," I said, "that would just be fantastic, you

know. Thanks in advance, Audie, really, I mean it, just for trying, I can't thank you enough. This place, well, it really sucks."

There it was, hanging out, my desperate and pathetic plea for help. Really, there was nowhere to go but down from there. Still, the silence stretched and snapped and I said, "Hey, speaking of, can I offer you guys a tour of the ward? I mean, it's not much, but it's home."

So I showed them: the droolers and the fondlers and the pukers and my horrible little room and the scarred Ping-Pong table and the sticky decks of cards and the meshed-in TV. Alphie actually seemed to dig it, in a kind of horrified way. He started comparing it to the new Kingston Pen, where he'd done his six-month bit. After seeing the first puker, Audie went quiet and thin-lipped, leaving nothing but Alphie's enthusiastic gurgling as counterpoint to my tour.

"Art," Audie said finally, desperately, "do you think they'd let us take you out for a cup of coffee or a walk around the grounds?"

I asked. The nurse looked at a comm for a while, then shook her head.

"Nope," I reported. "They need a day's notice of off-ward supervised excursions."

"Well, too bad," Audie said. I understood her strategy immediately. "Too bad. Nothing for it, then. Guess we should get back to our hotel." I planted a dry kiss on her cheek, shook Alphie's sweaty hand, and they were gone. I skipped supper that night and ate cookies until I couldn't eat another bite of rich chocolate.

"Got a comm?" I ask Doc Szandor, casually.

"What for?"

"Wanna get some of this down. The ideas for the hospital. Before I go back out on the ward." And it *is* what I want to do, mostly. But the temptation to just log on and do my thing—oh!

"Sure," he says, checking his watch. "I can probably stall them for a couple hours more. Feel free to make a call or whatever, too."

Doc Szandor's a good egg.

>>>>>>>>>>24

Father Ferlenghetti showed up at Art's Gran's at 7 PM, just as the sun began to set over the lake, and Art and he shared lemonade on Gran's sunporch and watched as the waves on Lake Ontario turned harshly golden.

"So, Arthur, tell me, what are you doing with your life?" the Father said. He had grown exquisitely aged, almost translucent, since Art had seen him last. In his dog collar and old-fashioned aviator's shades, he looked like a waxworks figure.

Art had forgotten all about the Father's visit until

Gran stepped out of her superheated kitchen to remind him. He'd hastily showered and changed into fresh slacks and a mostly clean tee shirt, and had agreed to entertain the priest while his Gran finished cooking supper. Now, he wished he'd signed up to do the cooking.

"I'm working in London," he said. "The same work as ever, but for an English firm."

"That's what your grandmother tells me. But is it making you happy? Is it what you plan to do with the rest of your life?"

"I guess so," Art said. "Sure."

"You don't sound so sure," Father Ferlenghetti said.

"Well, the *work* part's excellent. The politics are pretty ugly, though, to tell the truth."

"Ah. Well, we can't avoid politics, can we?"

"No, I guess we can't."

"Art, I've always known that you were a very smart young man, but being smart isn't the same as being happy. If you're very lucky, you'll get to be my age and you'll look back on your life and be glad you lived it."

Gran called him in for dinner before he could think of a reply. He settled down at the table and Gran handed him a pen.

"What's this for?" he asked.

"Sign the tablecloth," she said. "Write a little something and sign it and date it, nice and clear, please."

"Sign the tablecloth?"

"Yes. I've just started a fresh one. I have everyone sign my tablecloth and then I embroider the signatures in, so I have a record of everyone who's been here for supper. They'll make a nice heirloom for your children—I'll show you the old ones after we eat."

"What should I write?"

"It's up to you."

While Gran and the Father looked on, Art uncapped the felt-tip pen and thought and thought, his mind blank. Finally, he wrote, "For my Gran. No matter where I am, I know you're thinking of me." He signed it with a flourish.

"Lovely. Let's eat now."

Art meant to log in and see if Colonelonic had dredged up any intel on Linda's ex, but he found himself trapped on the sunporch with Gran and the Father and a small stack of linen tablecloths hairy with embroidered wishes. He traced their braille with his fingertips, recognizing the names of his childhood. Gran and the Father talked late into the night, and the next thing Art knew, Gran was shaking him awake. He was draped in a tablecloth that he'd pulled over himself like a blanket, and she folded it and put it away while he ungummed his eyes and staggered off to bed.

Audie called him early the next morning, waking him up.

"Hey, Art! It's your cousin!"

"Audie?"

"You don't have any other female cousins, so yes,

that's a good guess. Your Gran told me you were in Canada for a change."

"Yup, I am. Just for a little holiday."

"Well, it's been long enough. What do you do in London again?"

"I'm a consultant for Virgin/Deutsche Telekom." He has this part of the conversation every time he speaks with Audie. Somehow, the particulars of his job just couldn't seem to stick in her mind.

"What kind of consultant?"

"User experience. I help design their interactive stuff. How's Ottawa?"

"They pay you for that, huh? Well, nice work if you can get it."

Art believed that Audie was being sincere in her amazement at his niche in the working world, and not sneering at all. Still, he had to keep himself from saying something snide about the lack of tangible good resulting from keeping MPs up to date on the poleconomy of semiconductor production in PacRim sweatshops.

"They sure do. How's Ottawa?"

"Amazing. And why London? Can't you find work at home?"

"Yeah, I suppose I could. This just seemed like a good job at the time. How's Ottawa?

"Seemed, huh? You going to be moving back, then? Quitting?"

"Not anytime soon. How's Ottawa?"

"Ottawa? It's beautiful this time of year. Alphie

and Enoch and I were going to go to the trailer for the weekend, in Calabogie. You could drive up and meet us. Swim, hike. We've built a sweatlodge near the dock; you and Alphie could bake up together."

"Wow," Art said, wishing he had Audie's gift for changing the subject. "Sounds great. But. Well, you know. Gotta catch up with friends here in Toronto. It's been a while, you know. Well." The image of sharing a smoke-filled dome with Alphie's naked, cross-legged, sweat-slimed paunch had seared itself across his waking mind.

"No? Geez. Too bad. I'd really hoped that we could reconnect, you and me and Alphie. We really should spend some more time together, keep connected, you know?"

"Well," Art said. "Sure. Yes." Relations or no, Audie and Alphie were basically strangers to him, and it was beyond him why Audie thought they should be spending time together, but there it was. *Reconnect, keep connected.* Hippies. "We should. Next time I'm in Canada, for sure, we'll get together, I'll come to Ottawa. Maybe Christmas. Skating on the canal, OK?"

"Very good," Audie said. "I'll pencil you in for Christmas week. Here, I'll send you the wish lists for Alphie and Enoch and me, so you'll know what to get."

Xmas wishlists in July. Organized hippies! What planet did his cousins grow up on, anyway?

"Thanks, Audie. I'll put together a wishlist and pass it along to you soon, OK?" His bladder nagged at him. "I gotta run now, all right?"

"Great. Listen, Art, it's been, well, great to talk to you again. It really makes me feel whole to connect with you. Don't be a stranger, all right?"

"Yeah, OK! Nice to talk to you, too. Bye!"

"Safe travels and wishes fulfilled," Audie said.

"You too!"

>>>>>>>>>>25

Now I've got a comm, I hardly know what to do with it. Call Gran? Call Audie? Call Fede? Login to an EST chat and see who's up to what?

How about the Jersey clients?

There's an idea. Give them everything, all the notes I built for Fede and his damned patent application, sign over the exclusive rights to the patent for one dollar and services rendered (i.e., getting me a decent lawyer and springing me from this damned hole).

My last lawyer was a dickhead. He met me at the courtroom fifteen minutes before the hearing, in a private room whose fixtures had the sticky filthiness of a bus-station toilet. "Art, yes, hello, I'm Allan Mendelson, your attorney. How are you?

He was well over 6'6", but weighed no more than 120 lbs and hunched over his skinny ribs while he talked, dry-washing his hands. His suit looked like the kind of thing you'd see on a Picadilly Station homeless person, clean enough and well-enough fitting, but with an indefinable air of cheapness and falsehood.

"Well, not so good," I said. "They upped my meds this morning, so I'm pretty logy. Can't concentrate. They said it was to keep me calm while I was transported. Dirty trick, huh?"

"What?" he'd been browsing through his comm, tapping through what I assumed was my file. "No, no. It's perfectly standard. This isn't a trial, it's a hearing. We're all on the same side, here." He tapped some more. "Your side."

"Good," Art said. "My grandmother came down, and she wants to testify on my behalf."

"Oooh," the fixer said, shaking his head. "No, not a great idea. She's not a mental health professional, is she?"

"No," I said. "But she's known me all my life. She knows I'm not a danger to myself or others."

"Sorry, that's not appropriate. We all love our families, but the court wants to hear from people who have qualified opinions on this subject. Your doctors will speak, of course."

"Do I get to speak?"

"If you *really* want to. That's not a very good idea, either, though, I'm afraid. If the judge wants to hear from you, she'll address you. Otherwise, your best bet is to sit still, no fidgeting, look as sane and calm as you can."

I felt like I had bricks dangling from my limbs and

one stuck in my brain. The new meds painted the world with translucent whitewash, stuffed cotton in my ears and made my tongue thick. Slowly, my brain absorbed all of this.

"You mean that my Gran can't talk, I can't talk, and all the court hears is the doctors?"

"Don't be difficult, Art. This is a hearing to determine your competency. A group of talented mental health professionals have observed you for the past week and they've come to some conclusions based on those observations. If everyone who came before the court for a competency hearing brought out a bunch of irrelevant witnesses and made long speeches, the court calendar would be backlogged for decades. Then other people who were in for observation wouldn't be able to get their hearings. It wouldn't work for anyone. You see that, right?"

"Not really. I really think it would be better if I got to testify on my behalf. I have that right, don't I?"

He sighed and looked very put-upon. "If you insist, I'll call you to speak. But as your lawyer, it's my professional opinion that you should *not* do this."

"I really would prefer to."

He snapped his comm shut. "I'll meet you in the courtroom, then. The bailiff will take you in."

"Can you tell my Gran where I am? She's waiting in the court, I think."

"Sorry. I have other cases to cope with—I can't really play messenger, I'm afraid."

When he left the little office, I felt as though I'd

been switched off. The drugs weighted my eyelids and soothed my panic and outrage. Later, I'd be livid, but right then I could barely keep from folding my arms on the grimy table and resting my head on them.

The hearing went so fast I barely even noticed it. I sat with my lawyer and the doctors stood up and entered their reports into evidence—I don't think they read them aloud, even, just squirted them at the court reporter. My Gran sat behind me, on a chair that was separated from the court proper by a banister. She had her hand on my shoulder the whole time, and it felt like an anvil there to my dopey muscles.

"All right, Art," my jackass lawyer said, giving me a prod. "Here's your turn. Stand up and keep it brief."

I struggled to my feet. The judge was an Asian woman about my age, a small round head set atop a shapeless robe and perched on a high seat behind a high bench.

"Your Honor," I said. I didn't know what to say next. All my wonderful rhetoric had fled me. The judge looked at me briefly, then went back to tapping her comm. Maybe she was playing solitaire or looking at porn. "I asked to have a moment to address the Court. My lawyer suggested that I not do this, but I insisted.

"Here's the thing. There's no way for me to win here. There's a long story about how I got here. Basically, I had a disagreement with some of my coworkers who were doing something that I thought was immoral.

They decided that it would be best for their plans if I was out of the way for a little while, so that I couldn't screw them up, so they coopered this up, told the London police that I'd gone nuts.

"So I ended up in an institution here for observation, on the grounds that I was dangerously paranoid. When the people at the institution asked me about it, I told them what had happened. Because I was claiming that the people who had me locked up were conspiring to make me look paranoid, the doctors decided that I *was* paranoid. But tell me, how could I demonstrate my non-paranoia? I mean, as far as I can tell, the second I was put away for observation, I was guaranteed to be found wanting. Nothing I could have said or done would have made a difference."

The judge looked up from her comm and gave me another once-over. I was wearing my best day clothes, which were my basic London shabby chic white shirt and gray wool slacks and narrow blue tie. It looked natty enough in the UK, but I knew that in the US it made me look like an overaged door-to-door Mormon. The judge kept looking at me. *Call to action*, I thought. *End your speeches with a call to action*. It was another bit of goofy West Coast Vulcan Mind Control, courtesy of Linda's fucking ex.

"So here's what I wanted to do. I wanted to stand up here and let you know what had happened to me and ask you for advice. If we assume for the moment that I'm *not* crazy, how should I demonstrate that here in the court?"

The judge rolled her head from shoulder to shoulder, making glossy black waterfalls of her hair. The whole hearing is very fuzzy for me, but that hair! Who ever heard of a civil servant with good hair?

"Mr. Berry," she said, "I'm afraid I don't have much to tell you. It's my responsibility to listen to qualified testimony and make a ruling. You haven't presented any qualified testimony to support your position. In the absence of such testimony, my only option is to remand you into the custody of the Department of Mental Health until such time as a group of qualified professionals see fit to release you." I expected her to bang a gavel, but instead she just scritched at her comm and squirted the order at the court reporter and I was led away.

I didn't even have a chance to talk to Gran.

>>>>>>>>>>26

Received address book entry ''Toby Ginsburg'' from Colonelonic.

Colonelonic (private): This guy's up to something. Flew to Boston twice this week. Put a down payment on a house in Orange County. _Big_ house. _Big_ down payment. A car, too: vintage T-bird convertible. A gas burner! Bought CO_2 credits for an entire year to go with it.

Trepan: /private Colonelonic Huh. Who's he working for?

Colonelonic (private): Himself. He Federally incorpo-
rated last week, something called "TunePay, Inc."
He's the Chairman, but he's only a minority share-
holder. The rest of the common shares are held by a
dummy corporation in London. Couldn't get any details
on that without using a forensic accounting package,
and that'd get me fired right quick.

Trepan: /private Colonelonic It's OK. I get the picture. I
owe you one, all right?

Colonelonic (private): sweat.value==0 Are you going to
tell me what this is all about someday? Not some
bullshit about your girlfriend?

Trepan: /private Colonelonic Heh. That part was true, actually. I'll tell you the rest, maybe, someday. Not
today, though. I gotta go to London.

Art's vision throbbed with his pulse as he jammed his clothes back into his backpack with one hand while he booked a ticket to London on his comm with the other. Sweat beaded on his forehead as he ordered the taxi while scribbling a note to Gran on the smart-surface of her fridge.

He was verging on berserk by the time he hit airport security. The guard played the ultrasound flashlight over him and looked him up and down with his goggles, then had him walk through the chromatograph twice. Art tried to breathe calmly, but it wasn't happening. He'd take two deep breaths, think about how he was, yup, calming down, pretty good, especially since he was going to London to confront Fede about the fact that his friend had screwed him stabbed him in the back using his girlfriend to distract him and meanwhile she was in Los Angeles sleeping with her fucking ex who was going to steal his idea and sell it as his own that fucking prick boning his girl right then almost certainly laughing about poor old Art, dumb-fuck stuck in Toronto with his thumb up his ass, oh Fede was going to pay, that's right, he was—and then he'd be huffing down his nose, hyperventilating, really losing his shit right there.

The security guard finally asked him if he needed a doctor.

"No," Art said. "That's fine. I'm just upset. A friend of mine died suddenly and I'm flying to London for the funeral." The guard seemed satisfied with this explanation and let him pass, finally.

He fought the urge to get plastered on the flight and vibrated in his seat instead, jiggling his leg until his seatmate—an elderly businessman who'd spent the flight thus far wrinkling his brow at a series of spreadsheets on his comm—actually put a hand on Art's knee and said, "Switch off the motor, son. You're gonna burn it out if you idle it that high all the way to Gatwick."

Art nearly leapt out of his seat when the flight attendant wheeled up the duty-free cart, bristling with novelty beakers of fantastically old whiskey shaped like jigging Scotchmen and drunken lep-rechauns swinging from lampposts.

By the time he hit UK customs he was supersonic, ready to hammer an entire packet of Player's filterless into his face and light them with a blowtorch. It wasn't even 0600h GMT, and the Sikh working the booth looked three-quarters asleep under his turban, but he woke right up when Art stepped past the red line and slapped both palms on the counter and used them as a lever to support him as he pogoed in place.

"Your business in England, sir?"

"I work for Virgin/Deutsche Telekom. Let me beam you my visa." His hands were shaking so badly he dropped his comm to the hard floor with an ominous clatter. He snatched it up and rubbed at the fresh dent in the cover, then flipped it open and stabbed at it with a filthy fingernail.

"Thank you, sir. Door number two, please."

Art took one step towards the baggage carousel when the words registered. Customs search! God-fuckingdamnit! He jittered in the private interview room until another Customs officer showed up, over-rode his comm and read in his ID and credentials, then stared at them for a long moment.

"Are you quite all right, sir?"

"Just a little wound up," Art said, trying desperately to sound normal. He thought about telling the dead friend story again, but unlike a lowly airport security drone, the Customs man had the ability and inclination to actually verify it. "Too much coffee on the plane. Need to have a slash like you wouldn't believe."

The Customs man grimaced slightly, then chewed a corner of his little moustache. "Everything else is all right, though?"

"Everything's fine. Back from a business trip to the States and Canada, all jetlagged. You know. Can you believe the bastards actually expect me at the office today?" This might work. Piss and moan about the office until he gets bored and lets him go. "I mean, you work your guts out, fly halfway around the world and do it some more, get strapped into a torture seat—you think Virgin springs for business-class tickets for its employees? Hell no!—for six hours, then they want you at the goddamned office."

"Virgin?" the Customs man said, eyebrows going up. "But you flew in on BA, sir."

Shit. Of course he hadn't booked a Virgin flight. That's what Fede'd be expecting him to do, he'd be watching for Art to use his employee discount and hop a flight back. "Yes, can you believe it?" Art thought furiously. "They called me back suddenly, wouldn't even let me wait around for one of their own damned planes. One minute I'm eating breakfast, the next I'm in a taxi heading for the airport. I forgot half of my damned underwear in the hotel room! You'd think they could cope with *one little problem* without crawling up my cock, wouldn't you?"

"Sir, please, calm down." The Customs man looked alarmed and Art realized that he'd begun to pace.

"Sorry, sorry. It just sucks. Bad job. Time to quit, I think."

"I should think so," the Customs man said. "Welcome to England."

Traffic was early-morning light and the cabbie drove like a madman. Art kept flinching away from the oncoming traffic, already unaccustomed to driving on the wrong side of the road. England seemed filthy and gray and shabby to him now, tiny little cars with tiny, anal-retentive drivers filled with self-loathing, vegetarian meat-substitutes and bad dentistry. In his rooms in Camden Town, Art took a hasty and vengeful census of his stupid belongings, sagging rental furniture and bad art prints hanging askew (not any more, not after he smashed them to the floor). Bad English clothes (toss 'em onto the floor, looking for one thing he'd be caught dead wearing in NYC, and guess what, not a single thing). Stupid keepsakes from the Camden market, funny novelty lighters, retro rave flyers preserved in glassine envelopes.

He was about to overturn his ugly little pressboard coffee table when he realized that there was something on it.

A small, leather-worked box with a simple brass catch. Inside, the axe head. Two hundred thousand years old. Heavy with the weight of the ages. He hefted it in his hand. It felt ancient and lethal. He dropped it into his jacket pocket, instantly deforming the jacket into a stroke-y left-hanging slant. He kicked the coffee table over.

Time to go see Fede.

I have wished for a comm a hundred thousand times an hour since they stuck me in this shithole, and now that I have one, I don't know who to call. Not smart. Not happy.

I run my fingers over the keypad, think about all the stupid, terrible decisions that I made on the way to this place in my life. I feel like I could burst into tears, like I could tear the hair out of my head, like I could pound my fists bloody on the floor. My fingers, splayed over the keypad, tap out the old nervous rhythms of the phone numbers I've known all my life, my first house, my Mom's comm, Gran's place.

Gran. I tap out her number and hit the commit button. I put the phone to my head.

"Gran?"

"Arthur?"

"Oh, Gran!"

"Arthur, I'm so worried about you. I spoke to your cousins yesterday, they tell me you're not doing so good there."

"No, no I'm not." The stitches in my jaw throb in counterpoint with my back.

"I tried to explain it all to Father Ferlenghetti, but I

didn't have the details right. He said it didn't make any sense."

"It doesn't. They don't care. They've just put me here."

"He said that they should have let you put your own experts up when you had your hearing."

"Well, of *course* they should have."

"No, he said that they *had* to, that it was the law in Massachusetts. He used to live there, you know."

"I didn't know."

"Oh yes, he had a congregation in Newton. That was before he moved to Toronto. He seemed very sure of it."

"Why was he living in Newton?"

"Oh, he moved there after university. He's a Harvard man, you know."

"I think you've got that wrong. Harvard doesn't have a divinity school."

"It used to. And when he was done, he did another degree at Harvard, in psychiatry."

Oh, my.

"Oh, my."

"What is it, Arthur?"

"Do you have Father Ferlenghetti's number, Gran?"

Tonaishah's Kubrick-figure facepaint distorted into wild grimaces when Art banged into O'Malley House, raccoon-eyed with sleepdep, airline crud crusted at the corners of his lips, whole person quivering with righteous smitefulness. He commed the door savagely and yanked it so hard that the gas-lift snapped with a popping sound like a metal ruler being whacked on a desk. The door caromed back into his heel and nearly sent him sprawling, but he converted its momentum into a jog through the halls to his miniature office—the last three times he'd spoken to Fede, the bastard had been working out of his office—stealing his papers, no doubt, though that hadn't occurred to Art until his plane was somewhere over Ireland.

Fede was halfway out of Art's chair when Art bounded into the office. Fede's face was gratifyingly pale, his eyes thoroughly wide and scared. Art didn't bother to slow down, just slammed into Fede, bashing foreheads with him. Art smelled a puff of his own travel sweat and Fede's spicy Lilac Vegetal, saw blood welling from Fede's eyebrow.

"Hi, pal!" he said, kicking the door shut with a crash that resounded through the paper-thin walls.

"Art! Jesus fucking Christ, what the hell is wrong with you?" Fede backed away to the far corner of the office, sending Art's chair over backwards, wheels spinning, ergonomic adjustment knobs and rods sticking up in the air like the legs of an overturned beetle.

"TunePay, Inc.?" Art said, booting the chair into Fede's shins. "Is that the best fucking name you could come up with? Or did Toby and Linda cook it up?"

Fede held his hands out, palms first. "What are you talking about, buddy? What's wrong with you?"

Art shook his head slowly. "Come on, Fede, it's time to stop blowing smoke up my cock."

"I honestly have no idea—"

"Bullshit!" Art bellowed, closing up with Fede, getting close enough to see the flecks of spittle flying off his lips spatter Fede's face. "I've had enough bullshit, Fede!"

Abruptly, Fede lurched forward, sweeping Art's feet out from underneath him and landing on Art's chest seconds after Art slammed to the scratched and splintered hardwood floor. He pinned Art's arms under his knees, then leaned forward and crushed Art's windpipe with his forearm, bearing down.

"You dumb sack of shit," he hissed. "We were going to cut you in, after it was done. We knew you wouldn't go for it, but we were still going to cut you in—you think that was your little whore's idea? No, it was mine! I stuck up for you! But not anymore, you hear? Not anymore. You're through. Jesus, I gave you

212

this fucking job! I set up the deal in Cali. Fuck-off heaps of money! I'm through with you, now. You're done. I'm ratting you out to V/DT, and I'm flying to California tonight. Enjoy your deportation hearing, you dumb Canuck boy-scout."

Art's vision had contracted to a fuzzy black vignette with Fede's florid face in the center of it. He gasped convulsively, fighting for air. He felt his bladder go, and hot urine stream down his groin and over his thighs.

An instant later, Fede sprang back from him, face twisted in disgust, hands brushing at his urine-stained pants. "Damn it," he said, as Art rolled onto his side and retched. Art got up on all fours, then lurched erect. As he did, the axe head in his pocket swung wildly and knocked against the glass pane beside his office's door, spiderwebbing it with cracks.

Moving with dreamlike slowness, Art reached into his pocket, clasped the axe head, turned it in his hand so that the edge was pointing outwards. He lifted it out of his pocket and held his hand behind his back. He staggered to Fede, who was glaring at him, daring him to do something, his chest heaving.

Art windmilled his arm over his head and brought the axe head down solidly on Fede's head. It hit with an impact that jarred his arm to the shoulder, and he dropped the axe head to the floor, where it fell with a thud, crusted with blood and hair for the first time in 200,000 years.

Fede crumpled back into the office's wall, slid

down it into a sitting position. His eyes were open and staring. Blood streamed over his face.

Art looked at Fede in horrified fascination. He noticed that Fede was breathing shallowly, almost panting, and realized dimly that this meant he wasn't a murderer. He turned and fled the office, nearly bowling Tonaishah over in the corridor.

"Call an ambulance," he said, then shoved her aside and fled O'Malley House and disappeared into the Picadilly lunchtime crowd.

>>>>>>>>>>**29**

I am: sprung.

Father Ferlenghetti hasn't been licensed to practice psychiatry in Massachusetts for forty years, but the court gave him standing. The judge actually winked at me when he took the stand, and stopped scritching on her comm as the priest said a lot of fantastically embarrassing things about my general fitness for human consumption.

The sanatorium sent a single junior doc to my hearing, a kid so young I'd mistaken him for a hospital driver when he climbed into the van with me and gunned the engine. But no, he was a doctor who'd apparently been briefed on my case, though not very well. When the judge asked him if he had any opinions on Father Ferlenghetti's testimony, he fumbled with his comm while the Father stared at him through eyebrows thick enough to hide a hamster in, then finally stammered a few verbatim notes from my intake interview, blushed, and sat down.

"Thank you," the judge said, shaking her head as she said it. Gran, seated beside me, put one hand on my knee and one hand on the knee of Doc Szandor's brother-in-law, a hotshot Harvard Law post-doc whom we'd retained as corporate counsel for a new Limited Liability Corporation. We'd signed the articles of incorporation the day before, after Group. It was the last thing Doc Szandor did before resigning his post at the sanatorium to take up the position of Chief Medical Officer at HumanCare, LLC, a corporation with no assets, no employees, and a sheaf of shitkicking ideas for redesigning mental hospitals using off-the-shelf tech and a little bit of UE mojo.

>>>>>>>>>>30

Art was most of the way to the Tube when he ran into Lester. Literally.

Lester must have seen him coming, because he stepped right into Art's path from out of the crowd.

Art ploughed into him, bounced off of his dented armor, and would have fallen over had Lester not caught his arm and steadied him.

"Art, isn't it? How you doin', mate?"

Art gaped at him. He was thinner than he'd been when he tried to shake Art and Linda down in the doorway of the Boots, grimier and more desperate. His tone was just as bemused as ever, though. "Jesus Christ, Lester, not now, I'm in a hurry. You'll have to rob me later, all right?"

Lester chuckled wryly. "Still a clever bastard. You look like you're having some hard times, my old son. Maybe that you're not even worth robbing, eh?"

"Right. I'm skint. Sorry. Nice running into you, now I must be going." He tried to pull away, but Lester's fingers dug into his biceps, emphatically, painfully.

"Hear you ran into Tom, led him a merry chase. You know, I spent a whole week in the nick on account of you."

Art jerked his arm again, without effect. "You tried to rob me, Les. You knew the job was dangerous when you took it, all right? Now let me go—I've got a train to catch."

"Holidays? How sweet. Thought you were broke, though?"

A motorized scooter pulled up in the kerb lane beside them. It was piloted by a smart young police-woman with a silly foam helmet and outsized pads on her knees and elbows. She looked like the kid with the safety-obsessed mom who inflicts criminally dorky fashions on her daughter, making her the neighborhood laughingstock.

"Everything all right, gentlemen?"

Lester's eyes closed, and he sighed a put-upon sigh that was halfway to a groan.

"Oh, yes, Officer," Art said. "Peter and I were just making some plans to see our auntie for supper tonight."

Lester opened his eyes, then the corners of his mouth incremented upwards. "Yeah," he said. "'Sright. Cousin Alphonse is here all the way from Canada and Auntie's mad to cook him a proper English meal."

The policewoman sized them up, then shook her head. "Sir, begging your pardon, but I must tell you that we have clubs in London where a gentleman such as yourself can find a young companion, legally. We thoroughly discourage making such arrangements on the High Street. Just a word to the wise, all right?"

Art blushed to his eartips. "Thank you, Officer," he said with a weak smile. "I'll keep that in mind."

The constable gave Lester a hard look, then revved her scooter and pulled into traffic, her arm slicing the air in a sharp turn signal.

"Well," Lester said, once she was on the roundabout, "*Alphonse*, seems like you've got reason to avoid the law, too."

"Can't we just call it even? I did you a favor with the law, you leave me be?"

"Oh, I don't know. P'raps I should put in a call to our friend PC McGivens. He already thinks you're a dreadful tosser—if you've reason to avoid the law, McGivens'd be bad news indeed. And the police pay very well for the right information. I'm a little financially embarrassed, me, just at this moment."

"All right," Art said. "Fine. How about this: I will pay you 800 Euros, which I will withdraw from an Insta-Bank once I've got my ticket for the Chunnel train to Calais in hand and am ready to get onto the platform. I've got all of fifteen quid in my pocket right now. Take my wallet and you'll have cabfare home. Accompany me to the train and you'll get a month's rent, which is more than the police'll give you."

"Oh, you're a villain, you are. What is it that the police will want to talk to you about, then? I wouldn't want to be aiding and abetting a real criminal—could mean trouble."

"I beat the piss out of my coworker, Lester. Now, can we go? There's a plane in Paris I'm hoping to catch."

>>>>>>>>>>31

I have a brand-new translucent Sony Veddic, a series 12. I bought it on credit—not mine; mine's sunk, six months of living on plastic and kiting balance payments with new cards while getting the patents filed on the eight new gizmos that constitute HumanCare's sole asset has blackened my good name with the credit bureaus.

I bought it with the company credit card. The *company credit card*. Our local Baby Amex rep dropped it off himself after Doc Szandor faxed over the signed contract from the Bureau of Health. Half a million bucks for a proof-of-concept install at the very same Route 128 nuthatch where I'd been "treated." If that works, we'll be rolling out a dozen more installs over the next year: smart doors, public drug-prescription stats, locator bracelets that let "clients"—I've been learning the nuthouse jargon, and have forcibly removed "patient" from my vocabulary—discover other clients with similar treatment regimens on the ward, bells and whistles galore.

I am cruising the MassPike with HumanCare's first-ever employee, who is, in turn, holding on to HumanCare's first-ever paycheck. Caitlin's husband has been very patient over the past six months as she worked days fixing the ailing machinery at the sanatorium and nights prototyping my designs. He's been likewise patient with my presence on his sagging living-room sofa, where I've had my nightly ten-hour repose faithfully since my release. Caitlin and I have actually seen precious little of each other considering that I've been living under her roof. (Doc Szandor's Cambridge apartment is hardly bigger than my room at the hospital, and between his snoring and the hard floor, I didn't even last a whole night there.) We've communicated mostly by notes commed to her fridge and prototypes left atop my suitcase of day-clothes and sharp-edged toiletries at the foot of my makeshift bed when she staggered in from her workbench while I snored away the nights. Come to think of it, I haven't really seen much of Doc Szandor, either—he's been holed up in his rooms, chatting away on the EST channels.

I am well rested. I am happy. My back is loose and my Chi is flowing. I am driving my few belongings to a lovely two-bedroom—one to sleep in, one to work in—flat overlooking Harvard Square, where the pretty coeds and their shaggy boyfriends tease one another in the technical argot of a dozen abstruse disciplines. I'm looking forward to picking up a basic physics, law, medicine and business vocabulary just by sitting in my window with my comm, tapping away at new designs.

We drive up to a toll plaza and I crank the yielding, human-centric steering wheel toward the EZPass lane. The dealer installed the transponder and gave me a brochure explaining the Sony Family's approach to maximum driving convenience. But as I approach the toll gate, it stays steadfastly down.

The Veddic's HUD flashes an instruction to pull over to the booth. A bored attendant leans out of the toll booth and squirts his comm at me, and the HUD comes to life with an animated commercial for the new, improved TunePay service, now under direct MassPike management.

The TunePay scandal's been hot news for weeks now. Bribery, corruption, patent disputes—I'd been gratified to discover that my name had been removed from the patent applications, sparing me the nightly hounding Fede and Linda and her fucking ex had been subjected to on my comm as the legal net tightened around them.

I end up laughing so hard that Caitlin gets out of the car and walks around to my side, opens the door and pulls me bodily to the passenger side. She serenely ignores the blaring of the horns from the aggravated, psychotic Boston drivers stacked up behind us, walks back to the driver's side and takes the wheel.

"Thanks," I tell her, and lay a hand on her pudgy, freckled arm.

"You belong in a loony bin, you know that?" she says, punching me in the thigh harder than is strictly necessary.

"Oh, I know," I say, and dial up some music on the car stereo.

acknowledgments

This novel was workshopped by the Cecil Street Irregulars, the Novelettes, and the Gibraltar Point gang, and received excellent feedback from the first readers on the est-preview list (especially Pat York). I'm indebted to all the people who read and commented on this book along the way.

Thanks go to my editor, Patrick Nielsen Hayden, for reading this so quickly—minutes after I finished it! Likewise to my agent, Don Maass, thank you.

Thanks to Irene Gallo and Shelley Eshkar for knocking *two* out of the park with their cover designs for my books.

Thanks to my coeditors at Boing Boing and all the collaborators I've written with who've made me a better writer.

Thanks, I suppose, to the villains in my life, who inspired me to write this book rather than do something ugly that I'd regret.

Acknowledgments

Thanks to Paul Boutin for commissioning the *Wired* article of the same name.

Thanks to the readers and bloggers and Tribespeople who cared enough to check out my first book and liked it enough to check out this one.

Thanks to Creative Commons for the licenses that give me the freedom to say "Some Rights Reserved."

about the author

Cory Doctorow (www.craphound.com) is the author of *Down and Out in the Magic Kingdom, A Place So Foreign and Eight More,* and *The Complete Idiot's Guide to Publishing Science Fiction* (with Karl Schroeder). He was raised in Toronto and lives in San Francisco, where he works for the Electronic Frontier Foundation (www.eff.org), a civil liberties group. He's a journalist, editorialist, and blogger. Boing Boing (boingboing.net), the Weblog he coedits, is the most linked-to blog on the Net, according to Technorati. He won the John W. Campbell Award for Best New Writer at the 2000 Hugos. You can download the text of this book at craphound.com/est.